Spy for
—the—
Night Riders

Trailblazer Books

William & Catherine Booth ▪ *Kidnapped by River Rats*
Governor William Bradford ▪ *The Mayflower Secret*
John Bunyan ▪ *Traitor in the Tower*
Maude Cary ▪ *Risking the Forbidden Game*
Adoniram & Ann Judson ▪ *Imprisoned in the Golden City*
David Livingstone ▪ *Escape From the Slave Traders*
Martin Luther ▪ *Spy for the Night Riders*
Hudson Taylor ▪ *Shanghaied to China*
William Tyndale ▪ *The Queen's Smuggler*

*Trailblazers: Featuring Harriet Tubman
and Other Christian Heroes*

*Trailblazers: Featuring Amy Carmichael
and Other Christian Heroes*

*Trailblazers: Featuring William Tyndale
and Other Christian Heroes*

*Trailblazers: Featuring David Livingstone
and Other Christian Heroes*

*Trailblazers: Featuring Martin Luther
and Other Christian Heroes*

Heroes in Black History

*Hero Tales: A Family Treasury of True Stories
From the Lives of Christian Heroes* (Volumes I, II, & IV)

Spy for
– the –
Night Riders

Dave & Neta Jackson

Story illustrations by
Julian Jackson

BETHANY HOUSE PUBLISHERS
MINNEAPOLIS, MINNESOTA 55438

Published by Bethany House Publishers
11400 Hampshire Avenue South
Bloomington, Minnesota 55438

Bethany House Publishers is a division of
Baker Publishing Group, Grand Rapids, Michigan.

Printed in the United States of America by
Bethany Press International, Bloomington, MN.
September 2010, 20th printing

ISBN   978-1-55661-237-4

Library of Congress Cataloging-in-Publication Data

Jackson, Dave.
    Spy for the night riders / Dave and Neta Jackson.
        p.   cm. — (Trailblazer books)
    Summary: After coming to Wittenberg to seek an education,
Karl Schumacher becomes a student of Dr. Martin Luther, and
when the latter is declared a heretic, Karl accompanies him when
he travels to Worms to defend his views.

    [1. Reformation—Fiction.   2. Luther, Martin, 1483–1546—
Fiction.   3. Christian life—Fiction.]
I. Jackson, Neta.   II. Title.   III. Series.
PZ7.J132418Sp   1992
[Fic]—dc20   91–44063
    ISBN 1-55661-237-0   CIP
                                                         AC

All the adult characters in this book were real people, and the major events involving them are true with the exception of the escape down the Werra River.

In addition, Martin Luther *did* have two companions with him on his return from Worms. One was Brother John Petzensteiner. The other is unnamed in the historical records. Who knows? Maybe he was a young boy like our fictitious Karl Schumacher. In any case, it was this unnamed traveler who worked with the captain of the Wartburg Castle to arrange for Luther's abduction/rescue.

CONTENTS

DAVE AND NETA JACKSON are a full-time husband/ wife writing team who have authored and coauthored many books on marriage and family, the church, relationships, and other subjects. Their books for children include the TRAILBLAZER series and *Hero Tales* Volumes I, II, III, and IV. The Jacksons have two married children, Julian and Rachel, and make their home in Evanston, Illinois.

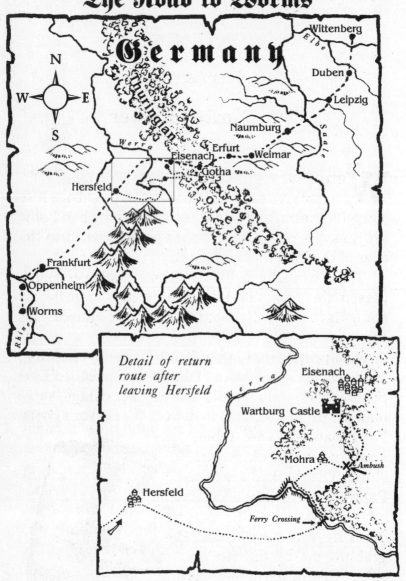

The Road to Worms

Germany

Wittenberg
Duben
Leipzig
Naumburg
Erfurt
Eisenach
Weimar
Gotha
Hersfeld
Frankfurt
Oppenheim
Worms

Thuringian
Forest

Werra
Elbe
Saale
Rhine

N
W — E
S

*Detail of return
route after
leaving Hersfeld*

Eisenach
Wartburg Castle
Mohra
Ambush
Hersfeld
Ferry Crossing
Werra

Chapter 1

The Wanted Poster

WHEN I WAS TEN YEARS OLD, I saw a burning.
Forgive me, but I need to tell you about it so you will understand why I got so scared when I saw my master's name on a wanted poster tacked to the door of the Wittenberg church.

That burning was the first time I had ever seen a person die. They said he was a *heretic*—that he did not believe the truth about God and the church. But I found it hard to believe.

It happened early on a cloudy Tuesday morning. My papa is a shoemaker. (That's why I'm called Karl Schumacher—you know, son of the village shoemaker.) He had sent me to deliver the mayor's boots. Papa had repaired them, and they were black and shiny. They looked great, as Papa's work always does. But when I knocked on the mayor's door, he was very upset. He grabbed me by the ear and said, "Get in here, boy, and

9

help me get the boots on. I haven't got all day. I can't be late for the burning."

I'd heard that there was going to be a burning, and I also knew that Mama wouldn't want me going near it. But I was curious, and I figured this was my chance to see one without her knowing. So I helped the mayor with his boots and then followed him to the town square in the center of our little village of Duben, Germany. There the constable had everything prepared, and a crowd had gathered. I tried to fade in among the other people hoping no one would notice me and tell Mama. As it turned out, everyone was so captivated by the burning that they probably wouldn't have noticed me even if I had stepped on their toes.

As soon as the mayor arrived, the constable struck a spark to the tinder of a huge woodpile and lit the fire. Then the two of them disappeared into the courthouse. They stayed there so long that I almost gave up and went home—Papa would be wondering why I was delayed. Even the fire would have burned down if several of the village people hadn't thrown more sticks on it. Someone in the growing crowd called, "Bring him out! We haven't got all day, ya know." Soon others picked up the cry until everyone was chanting, "Bring him out! Bring him out! Bring him out!" I was saying it too, but that was before I knew what a burning was like.

Some older boys, about fifteen (my age now), were standing nearby talking about burnings. "It's just like singeing the hair off hogs. 'Cept with a heretic, it ain't hair that gets burned away, it's heresy." They all laughed and pushed each other, pretending to throw one another into the fire.

Finally the mayor, the constable, and two helpers came out and ordered everyone to clear a path between the courthouse steps and the fire. At first nobody moved; everyone wanted a front row spot, I suppose. The constable had to poke them with the blunt end of his spear before they would move. Then the churchmen came out dressed in their fine red robes. I didn't know any of them. They were not from our town and had come as judges to conduct the heretic's trial. Finally the constable went back in and came out leading the heretic, whose hands were tied behind his back. Following them was our village priest, who looked in worse shape than the heretic—head hanging down, hair all mussed. He looked like a wild man.

I recognized the heretic as the man I'd seen preaching in the marketplace once or twice. He was also from out of town. People said he only came to our village to make converts.

He was tall and thin, with a long scraggly beard that grew mostly from his chin and very little on his cheeks. He didn't look nearly as old as Papa, but he was half bald. As he came down the steps and through the crowd, he gazed very calmly at all the people, and at one point he stared right at me and smiled. I can still see his eyes—deep-set and very light blue, almost chalk colored. I think . . . I hope I smiled back.

I had heard about people being "burned at the stake." But there was no stake for this burning. Instead the heretic was made to lie down with his back on an old ladder. There he was tied securely. The fire was again built up with fresh bundles of brush until it was roaring high.

All this time our village priest knelt beside the heretic. I was close enough to hear him pleading with the heretic to repent and save his life. When I looked, tears were pouring down our priest's face as he fumbled with the cross around his neck. It's hard to watch a grown-up cry. But the heretic just smiled and said, "I'm sorry, Father. I cannot unless I am shown by God's Word to be wrong." What he was supposed to be wrong about, I had no idea. To disagree with the church on anything was enough.

Then the constable and his men tipped the ladder up and balanced it on one end. The heretic was tied to the other end with his back toward the fire. It was shocking how he looked like Jesus Christ Himself as he hung there above the crowd. Then one of the judges asked if he had any final things to say and warned him that he could still save his life if he would change his mind.

The heretic looked around, and then shouted so loudly everyone could hear, "I have only this to say." And then he began to sing in as clear and beautiful a tenor voice as I've ever heard.

In thee, O Lord, do I put my trust.
Let me never be brought to confusion.

Deliver me in thy righteousness,
And forgive those who plot my ruin.

They allowed him to sing it twice, then let the ladder fall back so that the heretic landed squarely in the fire. Sparks flew up everywhere, and some of the burning sticks flipped out toward the crowd causing some people to jump back out of the way. But there in the flames, instead of screaming in pain, the heretic continued to sing until he had no more breath. And then, as the fire burned through the cords that bound his arms, he miraculously raised one hand toward heaven. It stayed there until it looked like a charred branch from an old tree.

I can tell you that the smell of burning flesh was something awful. I'll never forget it. In fact, I get sick just remembering it.

I learned from his execution that more than just bad people could be condemned here in Germany, or anywhere in the Holy Roman Empire for that matter. Anyone who could praise God while he burned and not curse those who had put him into the flames must have had the Spirit of Christ within him. And I think others felt the same. From the moment he began singing until we all drifted away to our homes, there was not one word spoken, not even by those older boys who thought they knew so much.

Ever since then, whenever anyone mentions the burning that happened in Duben, it's with the respect you'd expect for a saint—no mocking, no laughing. And our village priest? The next day he wandered off muttering to himself and has never been heard from since.

So now maybe you can understand why I got so worried when I saw my master's name on that wanted poster on the church door. In big, bold letters the poster called him *heretic*! But even though my master, Doctor Martin Luther, is one of the most famous teachers in the empire, that wouldn't keep him from burning if he were tried and convicted for heresy.

I don't live in my home town of Duben anymore. As the youngest son, there was no room for me in my father's shoe business, and I wanted an education rather than a trade, anyway. To get my education I came here to the German city of Wittenberg and asked Doctor Luther to take me on as his servant. I run his errands, keep his clothes and quarters clean, and serve as his stable boy when he travels. In return he lets me sit in on his lectures at the university, and he even tutors me in the evenings if he isn't too tired. It's the perfect situation for me. And maybe someday I'll even become a regular student.

But this particular day as I was coming down the street after returning a horse and a cart we had borrowed to visit some nearby villages, I noticed a new poster tacked to the church door. The poster wasn't a single sheet of paper. Actually, it was more like a booklet, what people call a *bull*. In Wittenberg that door is the city's most reliable source for news. All the official notices get put up there for everyone to read. That's the door where Doctor Luther posted his famous ninety-five theses three years ago; they were his arguments against the church's false doctrines and practices. The paper was his way of protesting the evil practices in the church and was saying they had to change. Of course, the church officials didn't like it.

But what caught my eye this time was my master's name. I read quickly. It was dated June 15, 1520—five months ago—and was from the pope, the top official of the Roman Catholic Church. It seemed to say that Doctor Luther would be kicked out of the church unless he went to Rome and repented of his *heretical* writings and ideas.

Go to Rome? Repent? That was just a nice way of saying that the church had already condemned him! I read on. The notice forbade anyone from defending Luther's writings or helping him in any way. My heart began beating faster. This was a formal Bull of Excommunication! He was being kicked out of the church, and anyone who helped him would be condemned too.

I tried to think through what this meant. Doctor Luther might be famous, and he might be a very good teacher, but unless he changed his mind about the importance of God's Word—and I knew he wouldn't—he wasn't safe.

I scanned the street to see if anyone was watching. People were going about their own business, not paying any attention to me . . . except for a girl about my age standing by a fruit stall in the street. I'd never seen her before. She was dressed better than a common peasant girl, but she carried a basket, so she had probably come to market. She had unusually long black hair that hung freely and waved in the breeze. Most girls her age covered their heads. *Enough of that*, I told myself. This was no time to gawk at a pretty girl. When she turned away, I tore the poster from the door and quickly rolled it up. Then I stuffed it inside my tunic as I raced toward the university.

My master was in danger. But in helping him, so was I.

Chapter 2

Risky Business

I FOUND DOCTOR LUTHER in the university square talking to some of his students about his afternoon lecture. As politely as I could, I interrupted them. "Please excuse me, sir. But I must have a word with you!"

He probably thought I'd had some problem returning the horse and cart and answered, "Don't worry about it, Karl. We'll talk about it tonight and get it all straightened out then. Now you go along and prepare something nice for my birthday." Then he smiled good-naturedly.

Oh, no. I'd completely forgotten! It was November 11, and—I figured quickly—Doctor Luther was thirty-seven years old. I was about to press my news, but he had already turned back to his students. So I left the square and hurried to the market, where I purchased some new candles, fresh bread, wine, cheese, and a small honey cake.

When I finally returned to our quarters, Doctor Luther was already there. I dumped my parcels on the table and quickly pulled out the bull. "I found this on the church door," I said.

Luther flattened out the booklet and began paging through it. "So John Eck has finally gone public, has he? It doesn't matter that the bull was already delivered to me privately."

"Then you've already seen it?" I asked.

"Yes, yes. It was presented to the headmaster of the university, and he showed it to me some time ago. But I should have known. Eck wouldn't miss the chance to stick it to me publicly."

John Eck is my master's chief enemy. I'd seen him once at the University of Leipzig, where he had opposed Luther in a public debate. Eck was a very determined and cunning man.

"So you think he did it?" I asked.

"Who else?" Luther tossed the papers onto the little pile on the floor beside his desk.

"Aren't you going to do anything about it?" I asked.

"What's there to do? Write another pamphlet telling why this is unfair?"

"Well, maybe. But . . . don't you have to go to Rome to defend yourself?"

"There's no defending myself against a charge like this in Rome. The pope issued the bull, though John Eck probably dictated the whole thing word-for-word. But when you're called to Rome, you either go and repent fully, making yourself look like a fool, or you . . ."

"Or you do what?"

"I don't know. But I'll think of something."

I stood looking at the paper on the floor, but Doctor Luther was rummaging in my parcels. So I tried to forget the threatening paper and what could come of it, turning my attention to my master's birthday celebration. Doctor Luther was quite merry and made a big show of cutting the honey cake.

After we'd eaten, I asked, "Doctor Luther, when you were a boy, what did you want to be when you grew up?"

"What did I want to be—what?—when I was your age?"

"Yeah. In my family, my parents always asked us on our birthdays: 'What do you want to be when you grow up?' So on their birthdays we'd ask them what they had wanted to be when they were our age—sort of a joke, I guess."

"Hmmm. I don't know." Doctor Luther scratched his chin. "I didn't want to be a miner like my father. His was a terrible life, breathing dust all day and coughing it up all night. I wanted to be something different. Maybe that's why I took a liking to you, Karl. I know what it's like to not follow in your father's footsteps. I admire you for wanting to do something different."

"But did you always want to be a teacher?"

"No, no." He laughed a little as he dipped his sweetcake in his cup of cider. "I guess as a boy I wanted to be a knight fighting for a powerful lord, defeating all the evil that threatened the land! In fact, there was an old folk hero named Knight George who freed his people from a cruel foreign king and won the land back for the rightful and true king. Did you ever hear that tale?"

I nodded. I'd heard it a time or two.

"Well, I wanted to be Knight George," grinned Doctor Luther. "What do you think of that?"

"I don't know," I smiled, trying to imagine the scholarly professor riding a charger and swinging a sword. But that night lying in my cot before I fell asleep, I couldn't help but think that Doctor Luther had become a kind of knight "fighting for the right." The church of Rome had become very corrupt. Many of the leaders didn't seem to care about helping people know God. All they wanted was to get people's money. And they did it any way they could—like selling *indulgences,* which were sheets of paper that said a person's sins were forgiven. This had made Doctor Luther very angry. He preached that forgiveness can't be bought and sold—it's a gift from God, received by faith when a person truly turns from their sin and asks God's forgiveness.

That's how John Eck became Luther's enemy. Eck defended these evil practices; Luther opposed them. I knew a real battle was brewing—not just between those two men but all across the church and throughout the empire. But because the Roman Catholic Church and the Holy Roman Empire stood together, people like Luther who were calling for the church to change its practices were said to be traitors.

But weeks passed and Doctor Luther did nothing about going to Rome as ordered by the pope. Then one day I overheard him talking with some of the other university professors. "I have appealed to the emperor," he said. He meant Charles the Fifth, the ruler of the entire Holy Roman Empire.

"You did *what?*" Brother Nicholas exclaimed. "Don't you think that's rather risky, Luther? If the emperor condemns you, it could mean the death sentence!" Nicholas von Amsdorf was a fellow monk and teacher who shared many of Luther's views—at least in private.

"That may be true," Luther said calmly, "and I have no faith in the emperor himself. We all know he's young and so weak in character that he's controlled by others, mostly the pope's men. But at least in that court I will get a fair hearing. Our German protector, John Frederick, sits on the council as duke of the state of Saxony. He, among others, will see to a fair trial."

Listening to my master, I still felt uneasy. I wasn't sure the Duke of Saxony liked Doctor Luther. Some said he did; some said he didn't. But . . . I'd also heard that he worked hard to protect all his citizens, and he was a very powerful lord. He would never allow one of his most popular professors to be condemned as a heretic without a fair trial. So maybe what Luther did was smart.

But early on the morning of December 10, as I walked to the university, I noticed a large crowd gathered around the university bulletin board. As I wedged my way close to the board, one of the students was reading aloud.

Let all who follow the true Gospel be present at nine o'clock outside the town walls, where books of ungodly papal decrees and false religious teachings will be burned just like the Apostle Paul burned the books of witchcraft in the city of Ephesus. For today the enemies of the Gospel have grown so bold as to daily burn the evangelical books of Luther. So come, pious and zealous youth, to this religious spectacle, for possibly now is the time when the Antichrist must be revealed!

Had Luther put up the notice or had someone else? "Or maybe," said one student, "an enemy has posted this challenge to get Doctor Luther in trouble."

"He can't get into any more trouble than he already is," said another. "Haven't you heard that he has been ordered to answer charges of heresy?"

We all crowded into Luther's classroom, and shifted impatiently as Doctor Luther proceeded with his lecture. But at the end of the morning lecture, Luther cleared up the mystery:

"My dear students. You know that my writings have been condemned by the pope. And, in some southern cities, the corrupt church leaders have taken the chill out of the fall air by burning my writings. Well, it's nearly winter here in the north. So if you have nothing better to do after class, I invite you to accompany me outside the town gate where we will have a little hand-warming party of our own. I intend to burn all these false writings and decrees from the pope." And he held up a pile of manuscripts and books.

A great cheer went up from the students. They were eager to put action to the teachings they had been hearing during the previous weeks. Like a school of minnows startled in a pool, they all broke and darted for the door. "Karl," said Doctor Luther, "help me gather up these writings."

Outside Wittenberg's Elster Gate, Luther encouraged the students to build a fire. Doctor Luther's classes were often attended by over three hundred students, but this afternoon the crowd was even larger. Others must have joined the crowd as we marched through the streets. Several other univer-

sity professors accompanied us.

When the fire was well lit, Luther picked up the writings one by one, announced what each one was, and then tossed it onto the fire. Then, lifting high the bull calling him to come to Rome and renounce his writings and beliefs, Luther said, "Some of you have heard that I have been served with a Bull of Excommunication. If I do not recant of my beliefs and writings, I am to be thrown out of the Roman church. However, because the pope has brought down the truth of God, I also throw down this bull into the fire today. Amen!" The crowd cheered.

After that Luther and the other faculty members walked solemnly back to the university. But the students remained, and in a few minutes they were singing and dancing around the bonfire. Soon a kind of wildness took over the crowd . . . but it reminded me of the other burning I had witnessed as a young boy, so I just watched.

To my surprise, at the edge of the crowd, I noticed the same girl I'd seen near the church door the day I'd torn down the bull. This time her long dark hair was tied back at the nape of her neck, but it was still uncovered. And though her clothes were rather plain, her face had a beauty so serene that I doubted whether a thunderstorm could disturb it. She stood quietly as though she was . . . as though she was a "watcher." I can't think of a better word for it. It seemed that was her job—watching. And in response, I couldn't help but watch her. However, when our eyes met, she looked quickly away. Why look away when nothing else bothered her? And why wasn't she joining in the merriment? Did the fire remind her of something unpleasant, like it did me, or did she hold back for some other reason?

"Let's collect all the false writings in the whole town," shouted one student. As if on cue, the crowd swarmed back through the city gates. Soon someone produced an old cart that several mounted while others pulled it. Another student had a trumpet and began blasting off-key notes as the procession went through the streets. As the mob got rowdier, they began banging on people's doors demanding: "Do you have any of the pope's poison papers here? We intend to purge the town."

I had followed them down three streets and returned once to the bonfire to burn some more papers when I noticed the girl with the long dark hair leave the others. I probably wouldn't have paid any attention, but she looked all around as if checking to see if anyone noticed; then she ducked down a dingy alley. When I got to the same alley and glanced down it, she was running and had nearly reached the other end. Not very thrilled with the mood of the mob, I decided to follow her. After all, she was very pretty, and mysterious . . . why not find out where she lived?

I barely managed to keep her in sight. But after several turns she entered Raven's Tavern. Raven's Tavern? Why would she go in there? That's not where a family would live. Only strangers rented rooms there.

I stood outside trying to work up courage to go in

and explore when the door suddenly swung open and two men came out talking excitedly to each other. I recognized one: John Eck, Doctor Luther's enemy!

I started to turn around and walk away, but then I realized that Eck would not recognize me. So I just leaned against the tavern, crossed my arms and looked down the street like I was waiting for someone. But what I heard was startling.

"If Luther burned the pope's bull, then I must return to Rome at once," said Eck.

"Brother John, you know that wasn't the pope's bull," laughed the other man. "We wrote every word of it ourselves. The pope just signed it."

"That makes it the *pope's* bull. Now go to the stable and get us horses. I'll be along shortly," Eck said as he turned and walked down the street.

I couldn't believe it. That girl, the watcher, must have been a spy for Eck! The first time I had seen her was the day the bull was posted on the church door. Now she'd gone straight to the tavern, and in just a few minutes Eck knew what Doctor Luther had done and was preparing to leave for Rome!

I returned immediately to the university and

reported to Master Luther. He listened soberly, but all he said was, "There's no way to stop Eck from doing the Devil's bidding. The matter is clearly in God's hands. But it's those rampaging students that bother me! What did you say they were doing?"

As I told him again about the raid on the town, I could see Luther's displeasure. The next day in class, he lectured his students soundly: "Do you know what you're doing? You had no business accosting the townspeople. This fight against false religion isn't for fun and games! The mood in the land is very dark and dangerous; it could end in death for each of us."

A chill ran down my spine. I hoped Doctor Luther was wrong.

Chapter 3

No Time for Quitters

TWICE IN THE NEXT FEW WEEKS I was surprised to see "The Watcher," as I had come to call her. I thought she would have gone with John Eck back to Rome. Had Eck left her behind to spy on Doctor Luther? On the other hand, if that was what she was doing, why didn't I see her more often?

The first time I spotted her was on Christmas Day and quite by accident. Doctor Luther was preaching in the Castle Church, and she was right there in the congregation. I could hardly believe my eyes. A black lace veil partially covered her face, but it was her—no doubt about it.

After that I made it a practice to watch for her. At various times I would step quickly to our window and survey all the people in the commons down below. But she was never there. All I saw were the regular students and professors or special visitors to the university. I tried this evening and morning and midday. Always the same. If she was watching our quarters, I never saw her.

Whenever I was out with Doctor Luther, I would

glance behind us to catch her if she was following us. This created something of a problem as I kept bumping into things or into my master if he stopped or turned for some reason. The funny thing is, that's when I saw her again.

We were going to the printer's to pick up some fresh copies of Luther's popular little pamphlet, *The Freedom of a Christian*. Occasionally I would turn around and walk backwards for a few steps. Well, we were just passing Raven's Tavern when the door flew open, and I nearly smashed into The Watcher. I stumbled and nearly fell down. Then I felt so foolish

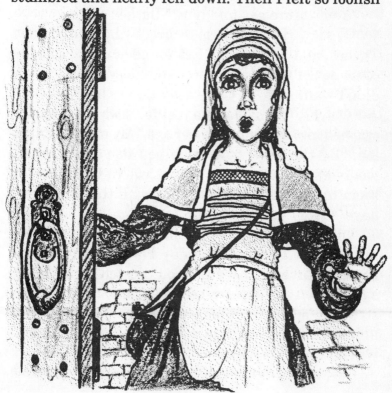

that I couldn't think of anything to say, but when Doctor Luther spoke for me and said, "Please excuse us," the girl turned and ran off as fast as possible. It seemed like she didn't want us to take any more notice of her than we already had.

"That's the girl," I said to my master as soon as she was out of earshot. "That's The Watcher."

"The who?"

"The girl who's spying on you for John Eck—the one I told you about on the day you burned the bull. She's the one who told Eck just before he left for Rome."

"You're sure *she* told him?" Luther said.

"Well . . . I saw her come directly here to Raven's Tavern, and that's when Eck found out. You saw her come out of there just now. And did you notice, she didn't want us to pay any attention to her?"

"Maybe. Or maybe she just felt awkward having crashed into a young man her age." My master chuckled. "By the way, how come you don't look where you're going—or else go where you're looking? You seem to be stumbling into things all the time these days."

I didn't see the girl for quite some time after that, but I didn't give up. One day I was on my way to Raven's Tavern to see if I could catch sight of her again when a finely dressed man came riding up the street on a great white, prancing horse. He carried an imperial banner, which could only mean that he was on royal business.

Just after passing me, he pulled up and addressed

all the people along the street who had stopped to stare at him. "I am Casper Sturm, imperial herald of His Majesty, Charles the Fifth, Sovereign of the Holy Roman Empire!" he announced haughtily as he surveyed the people. He looked down on us not only because he sat on a high horse, but as though he considered us commoners beneath his dignity. "Can one of you loyal citizens direct me to a certain Doctor Martin Luther?"

I hardly knew what to say. The emperor had a message for my master, a message so important that he had sent his herald to deliver it! While I stood there considering whether this was a great honor or a dangerous threat, two or three people stepped forward and tried to give the herald directions to the university. Finally I gathered my wits and said, "I'll take you there, your majesty. I work for Doctor Luther."

He turned in his saddle and said, "I am not 'his majesty,' young man. But if you can take me to Luther, I'll excuse your ignorance. Lead on. I've had a long ride and am eager to be off this beast."

My master was still giving his afternoon lecture—one on the evils of indulgences that I'd heard three times before (which is why I'd skipped the class). The herald didn't wait for him to conclude but marched right in. "Are you Martin Luther?" he interrupted. The students stared.

"I am."

"I am Casper Sturm, imperial herald of His Majesty, Charles the Fifth, Sovereign of the Holy Roman

Empire. You are to appear before the Imperial Council within twenty-one days. The Imperial Council is already in session in the city of Worms."

"And for what reason am I requested to appear?" asked Luther calmly.

"You are not *requested* to appear," the imperial herald said, looking at Doctor Luther out of the corner of his eyes. "You are *required* to appear to be tried on the charge of heresy. John Frederick, Duke of Saxony, has arranged for you to be guaranteed safe passage. That means I have 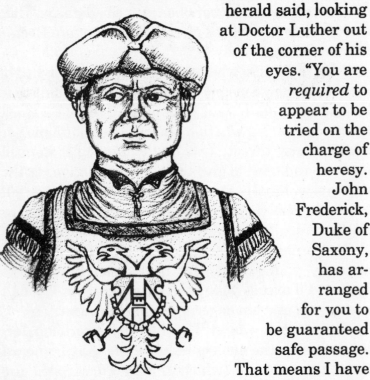 the sorry task of accompanying you to Worms. We leave in the morning."

"I can't possibly leave tomorrow," Doctor Luther protested. "I have far too much to do to get ready. Besides, if I have twenty-one days, it doesn't take that long to get to Worms. How about next . . ."

Luther stroked his clean-shaven chin. "How about next Tuesday?" Tuesday was four days away.

"*You* may have twenty-one days to arrive at Worms," said the imperial herald, "but I don't. You're coming with me. We leave in the morning."

With that the herald turned on the heels of his fine riding boots and marched out of the classroom. I had to jump out of the doorway or I think he would have walked right over me.

The students sat in stunned silence. I thought Doctor Luther would rush to get ready, but instead he said, "Let's see, where was I? Oh, yes. . . ." And he continued his lecture. I closed the door and walked in a daze back to our quarters, not even noticing the swirling snowflakes that began to sting my cheeks.

The more I thought about it, the more it looked like the end of my education. My master was leaving Wittenberg. And even if he prevailed at his trial and didn't get condemned to death (which was the most likely outcome), the trial could last for months. Even with the best outcome, there almost certainly would be a prison sentence—for years, probably. Maybe if I served him in prison, he could continue instructing me. . . .

I shook my head to clear it. What was I thinking of? Doctor Luther's *life* was at stake, and I was trying to figure out a way to get a little more education. How could I be so selfish? No, it would be best if I returned to my village and took up the family trade of shoemaking. That's where I belonged. Maybe, though—maybe I could travel with Doctor Luther for a day or so. Most likely he'd be going right through my little village of Duben.

Just as I was about to turn into the little stairway that led up to our rooms, I looked back over my shoulder—out of habit, I guess. And there she was. The Watcher was just coming around the corner, the same way I had come. When I stopped, she jumped back out of sight. Even through the swirling snow, I was sure it was her.

When Luther got home, his first words were, "Well, Karl, have you got my things packed?"

"No. But I'll get right to it."

"No need to rush," said Luther. "I talked to Sturm again and convinced him to wait a few days before we leave."

I let out a sigh of relief. I had a few more days before having to say good-bye. "How'd you do that?"

"I told him we have no way to travel. Unless he wants to pile the three of us on that big horse of his, he'll have to wait until we can arrange some kind of conveyance."

"The three of us?" I asked.

"Yes. Brother Nicholas has agreed to come with us. And his support will be such a comfort. Not that I don't value you, Karl, but Nicholas, being a fellow monk, will lend a degree of . . . oh, I don't know. I'll be glad for you both."

"Both? You want me to come, too?"

"Of course! You aren't thinking of quitting on me just when I need you most, are you?"

Chapter 4

Night Rider

ALMOST A WEEK PASSED before all the arrangements were made. And it was the good people of Wittenberg who finally made possible our transport. An old wagon and three horses were donated along with a considerable collection of funds to help pay for our lodging along the way.

Early on Tuesday morning, April 2, our party rambled out the city gate and pulled onto the ferry to cross the Elbe River. What a sight we must have been. Astride his powerful horse rode Casper Sturm, dressed in his imperial finery. His horse pranced impatiently as its great hooves thudded on the ferry deck.

Down the bank creaked our wagon, drawn by two horses and trailing the spare. Doctor Luther was in his professor's robe. Nicholas von Amsdorf was in his brown monk's habit. I was driving the wagon, wearing a beautiful green wool cape, a far better garment than I had ever owned. It had been donated for our trip by a town merchant. The three of us were perched atop our wagon, hanging on tight lest we be pitched off by every rock or rut.

Quite a crowd turned out to see us off, and who knows how far they would have followed along if it hadn't been for the river. Some students tried to negotiate a free passage from the ferryman: "But we're not going anywhere. We just want to see Doctor Luther off. We'll ride back on your return trip, so there's no need for us to pay."

"Goin' across and comin' straight back don't make it any easier to pull this ferry across," the ferryman grumbled. "Fact is, our load is too heavy all ready. I wouldn't take you even if you paid double toll."

The ferry was pulled across the river by means of a rope stretched from one bank to the other. The rope ran through guides on the raft as well as through one end of a wooden lever, about three feet long, called a "come-along." When the ferryman pulled on the lever, it bound the rope, giving him a good grip. By this means he pulled the raft as far as he could walk along its deck. Then he would loosen the come-along and slide it back up the rope for another bite.

We had just moved away from the shore when the ferryman turned and pointed at me. "You there, boy. Get down off that wagon and block your wheels. And keep those nags steady. I don't want them moving side to side, or we'll all take a drink."

And he was right, too. Halfway across, the spare horse started switching its tail and stamping one of its rear feet to shake off a horsefly. Each time it stamped its hoof, it moved over a few inches to a new position. Soon it was standing sideways to the wagon, and the upstream side of the ferry dipped down so that water began washing up over the deck. Just then an eddy in the river's current caught us and pushed that side lower still as the water washed higher.

"Quick, get that horse back to the center," yelled the ferryman as he pulled with all his might on his come-along to move us out of the fast current.

I splashed down the side of the ferry, already three or four inches under water and gave the horse a big shove. That nag must have realized she was on unsteady footing, because she didn't even push back but stepped right over.

Slowly the low side of the ferry rose, the flood retreated over the edge, and we were stable once more, or at least as stable as we could be.

The moment we touched the ground on the other side, Casper Sturm spurred his horse up the steep bank. But with the load on the front end suddenly reduced, the ferry bobbed up and freed itself from the muddy bank. The ferryman hadn't yet secured his rope, so the current started swinging us around. He cut loose with a string of swear words that would rot your teeth. "Get over here, kid, and give me a hand with this rope," he yelled, as though it had been my fault. I felt awful until I noticed him tossing angry looks in Sturm's direction. The ferryman didn't say anything to Sturm—the herald represented the emperor, after all—but it made me feel better to realize he wasn't really blaming me.

When we finally had the wagon up the bank, we

stopped a moment and looked back toward Wittenberg. It seemed so far away . . . like we'd been gone a week already.

As the day wore on, Brother Nicholas took a turn driving the wagon while I crawled back on top of our luggage. Doctor Luther had brought his lute, and

played and sang to us from time to time. I sat staring at the passing forest and small farms.

Casper Sturm rode ahead, supposedly to ensure our safe passage. There were robbers in the forest, but since they were outlaws anyway, I couldn't see what good one man could do if a band of them attacked. The imperial herald carried a small sword, but it wasn't like he was a knight or something. "It's not robbers he's protecting us from," explained Luther. "We don't have anything worth stealing anyway. He's protecting us from those in the Roman church who would like to do me in."

"You mean John Eck?" I asked, as I took off my cape. The day was starting to warm up.

"Well, I'm not sure he'd stoop to murder on his own. But there are others, even others he might hire."

"But why would your enemies want to attack you when they have already succeeded in bringing you to trial?" Then without thinking I said, "They're likely to get you anyway."

Luther leaned back and laughed. "You sure don't have much faith, do you, Karl? That's all right. That's all right. That could well be the outcome. I have faced it squarely. But to answer your question. There are many who *don't* want me to testify in Worms. No matter what happens to me, my trial could be the most important sermon I will ever preach. Never again am I likely to have an audience like this one."

"What do you mean?" I asked, trying to find a more comfortable position among our few bags and supplies.

"This Imperial Council is shaping up to be the most important conference ever held in Europe. Charles the Fifth is finally bringing more states together in the Holy Roman Empire than ever before. The Roman church, of course, is fighting to maintain control. But my booklet, *Address to the Christian Nobility*, has caused the princes from all the states to ask whether they really want to be under that much control by the Roman church. And the people are sick of the priests' greed and cruel use of church law."

The wagon creaked loudly as Luther continued. "All winter the roads were full of travelers going to Worms. You've seen some of them yourself coming through Wittenberg. I heard that William, duke of Bavaria, took five-hundred horsemen with him; Philip, the prince of Baden, had six-hundred. All the great bishops will be there as well as the knights, lesser nobility, representatives of cities, and many lawyers from the universities. Already the ambassadors from England, France, Venice, Poland, and Hungary have arrived."

"How will everyone fit in the council?" I asked, realizing as soon as I said it that it was a foolish question.

"Only designated delegates will be in the meetings, and only the meetings to which they have been invited. The more important question is," Luther winked at me, "where will they all stay in the little city of Worms? We may find ourselves sleeping under a tree outside town!"

"But why would so many people come if they can't be part of the meetings?"

"To be where the action is. The printers will be the ones getting rich on this council. Every day papers will be published on what has happened. They will be posted everywhere. People will get the news of the events that are shaping our world almost as soon as it happens from these . . . these newspapers."

We rode in silence for a while. Then Luther said, "Whether I am condemned or freed, the whole world will hear the truth. That's why I want to be there. But it is for that very reason that some of my enemies don't want me to testify."

I looked up at Casper Sturm, riding ahead to protect us from Luther's enemies. He was asleep in the saddle, his head hanging down and bobbing along with the plodding steps of his horse. Luther must have guessed what I was thinking—that Sturm didn't look very fierce at the moment. "No, Karl. His defense of us does not come from his ability to fight but from his position. He's the *imperial* herald. If he or anyone in his charge were harmed, the imperial army would be after them."

At midday we stopped by a small stream to water our horses and eat some bread and cheese. We weren't that far from my village. I knew this valley, and Duben was only over the next ridge.

When we got underway again, I asked if I could take the spare horse and ride on ahead. Doctor Luther said that would be fine. As I jumped on the horse and trotted off, Casper Sturm called after me: "Hey, boy, reserve me the best room in the best tavern in town."

"Yes, sir," I called back, knowing my assignment was easy. There is only one tavern in Duben, and it has only two rooms—both the same, as far as I knew.

That old nag gave me one of the roughest rides I've ever had. Trotting down the hill into Duben an hour later was like sliding down a steep mountain stream over rocks, sitting down.

I hadn't been home since last summer, and

Mother was wild with joy when I surprised her and Father by walking right into the house. She kept trying to hug and kiss me like I was still a little boy. I don't know, sometimes the way a mother can act makes a fellow feel like the only safe way to meet her is on opposite sides of a creek too deep to wade.

But as soon as Mother found out that Doctor Luther, Brother Nicholas, and the imperial herald were following behind, all my troubles with her fussing over me ended. She immediately began bustling about fixing a fine meal to feed us all. I tried to tell her that Casper Sturm would be going to the tavern, but she said, "He can't eat there. The food is terrible. Besides, it's probably been ages since he had a home-cooked meal." Then Mother assigned everyone jobs: I was to go reserve the room for Casper Sturm. Father was sent out to kill a couple of chickens and pluck them. (Mother doesn't usually order Father around, but this was a special situation, and he went off in good humor.) My sister, one year older and still living at home, fixed a place for Doctor Luther and Brother Nicholas to sleep. I thought that they'd probably stay with our church priest, but Mother wouldn't hear of it.

That evening after our meal—which Casper Sturm gladly accepted, to my surprise—Father started asking about the purpose of our trip. The more Luther said, the quieter Father got. I could see he didn't approve, so I jumped right in to defend the good work that Doctor Luther was doing. I was carrying on like a defense lawyer when Father interrupted. "Karl, I fully support the views of Doctor Luther. And," he continued, turning to Luther, "I have read every book of yours that I can find. My concern is with Karl's safety. This trip could be very dangerous, couldn't it?"

"I don't think it will be dangerous for Karl," said Brother Nicholas. "After all, he is not responsible for Martin Luther's ideas or writings. On this trip he's merely a stable boy."

"That's not entirely right," said Luther, holding up his hands as though to stop Brother Nicholas. "There could be danger. That I'll admit. The pope's bull warned of severe consequences to anyone who supports me. If the emperor and the imperial council rule against me and take a nasty turn, they could strike out against all who help me."

"Could that include Karl?" asked my mother. "He's only a boy."

"When the name 'heretic' starts getting thrown about, it can stick to anyone," Luther said.

"Then I don't want Karl going along," said Mother. "Two grown men ought to be capable of caring for their own horses and driving a wagon. You don't need a boy along."

"You are quite correct," said Luther. "And we wouldn't want to take him along against your wishes."

"But Mother, I want to go!" I protested. "No one is forcing me to go. I want to continue my education. And just today Doctor Luther was telling me about what an important council this will be. I may be able

43

to see many of the most important people in the whole world. Besides," I carried on, revealing my little plan, "even if Doctor Luther is sent to prison, I could still serve him—he will need someone to run his errands and bring supplies—and he could tutor me there. I'd learn even more."

When I finally shut up, I felt heat rising up my neck and knew I was turning red. There I'd gone and let everyone know how much more I was thinking of my own welfare than of Doctor Luther's. But for the moment, no one else seemed to notice.

"But our good doctor *could* be sentenced to death," said my father solemnly. "Still . . . I think it should be Karl's decision if Doctor Luther is inviting him."

44

"Oh, I am," assured Luther. "I would welcome his company and service. I think we will have good use for him. And I'll do my best to make sure that he remains safe. But the truth is, in this situation, I can make no guarantees."

"Well, then," concluded my father, "sleep on it tonight, Karl. But don't forget your mother's wisdom and feelings."

That settled it for me. There wasn't anything to think about; come morning, I'd be off down the road in that creaky old wagon.

Doctor Luther and Brother Nicholas were to sleep inside near the hearth, and that left little room for me. So I decided to curl up in the hay in our barn. The hayloft had often been a favorite place to be by myself when I was a small boy. But when I went out to get my green cape from the wagon—it would provide welcome warmth against the April night chill—someone on horseback took off galloping down the street.

Whoever it was had stopped by our wagon! I ran out to see if anything was missing. As I gazed into the gloom of the moonlit night, trying to make out the rider on the retreating horse, I thought I saw long flowing hair streaming out behind the rider's head.

Chapter 5

The Triumphal Entry

WAS IT THE GIRL, The Watcher? I tore off down the street as fast as I could go. I'd heard a fast runner can sometimes beat a horse. But that's only when the person and the horse have an equal start and the distance is very short.

Our village is small, and soon I pulled up winded at the edge of town. I was just able to hear the faint thumpity-thump of the horse's hooves disappearing on down the road—the road to Leipzig that we'd be taking the next morning.

I turned and walked slowly home. Was it The Watcher? How could it be? What would a young girl be doing riding alone, let alone galloping through the night? It just didn't make sense. If it was the girl, there didn't seem to be any reason for her to follow us. Eck, who was probably already in Worms, certainly had learned by other means that we were coming. Many people would travel faster than our slow wagon. They could tell him that we were on our way.

And if, as Luther had hinted, Eck wanted to

arrange for a band of robbers to attack us on the highway and prevent Luther from making it to Worms, what good could a girl do? She couldn't swing a sword in combat.

Then it came to me. Eck needed a special messenger. That's why she was hurrying on ahead. Eck couldn't wait for casual travelers to bring him news that we were on the way. He needed to know early so that he *could* arrange a trap.

I picked up my pace, intent on getting back home to warn Luther. But then I paused. Who would believe me? I hadn't actually seen the rider. I didn't know for sure it was the girl. And even if my story was believed, my parents might just use it and the new danger it represented to say I couldn't go. No. I'd wait. Tomorrow, once we were on the road, would be plenty of time to tell Luther.

In the morning I said good-bye to my folks, and I tried to reassure my mother that everything would be all right. She gave me a hug that I thought wouldn't quit, but finally she let me go and wiped a tear from her eye. "You be good, Karl, and I'll pray for you." Then we were off.

But by the light of morning, my story about the night rider seemed even more unbelievable. "When I came out to get my cape from the wagon last night," I said as the wagon rolled out of town, "there was a rider." I paused, but no one responded. "The rider was stopped right by our wagon . . . looking in." Still no one seemed interested enough to ask who the rider was.

"I think it was a spy," I said.

Brother Nicholas, who was driving again, turned and looked at me quizzically. But then he shook his head and turned back to staring at the road, or rather the rear end of Casper Sturm's fine horse.

"As soon as I came out, the rider took off and galloped all the way out of town."

Finally, Doctor Luther responded. "Now I know this is a small town, Karl, but it's not so small that you can see all the way from one end to the other. How do you know the rider galloped all the way out of town?" Luther asked just like the lawyer trying to teach one of his students to think more logically. "Maybe the person lives on the other side of town and turned in at home." He thought he had me.

"I know she left town because I followed her."

"Her?" challenged Brother Nicholas. "What's a woman doing riding around in the middle of the night? You must have been dreaming."

"I wasn't dreaming," I said. "It was The Watcher. And you know what I think she was doing . . ." Then I stopped. Doctor Luther's eyes narrowed as though he found my story quite ridiculous. I too began to see that my theory was pretty farfetched. Bad things *do* seem so much tamer by the light of day. So instead of telling them about the ambush I had imagined the night before, I just said, "Well, I think it was that girl. It kind of looked like her."

No one asked what I thought she was doing, so I didn't say any more. But I decided to keep a sharp eye out during the rest of the trip, and if I saw her again or if I saw anything suspicious, then I would tell everyone my theory.

That afternoon we arrived in Leipzig. It had been at the University of Leipzig that Martin Luther and John Eck had held their fiery public debates. The university and the city had mostly supported Eck, so we were wary and hoped to enter the city unnoticed—at least as unnoticed as one could with an imperial herald riding in front of your wagon.

But we had no such luck. It seemed everyone in town knew we were coming and had turned out to meet us. Most were friendly, though. And the city council officially welcomed Doctor Luther by giving him the traditional cup of wine when we reached the city. I think Casper Sturm felt a little jealous. Usually *he* is the person who gets honored upon entering a city.

We spent the night in rooms provided at the university. But when I was trying to fall asleep, I started thinking: How had everybody known that we were coming . . . and just when we would be arriving?

There had been other travelers on the road, and one or two had passed us. But I couldn't remember that they had recognized us. So how had the City of

Leipzig—Eck's old stomping grounds—known when we would arrive? It made me suspicious. Maybe that girl had announced us. And why had Luther's "enemy" city welcomed us so warmly? It felt like a set-up.

When the next day came, however, I still didn't say anything about my theories.

Leipzig was as far to the south as I had ever been, so the countryside was all new to me in the days that followed. I loved it—beautiful hills, rich forests, and snug farms and villages nestled in the ends of the green valleys. From Leipzig our road led southwest to Naumburg, picturesquely clustered about its great cathedral in the valley of the Saale River. Then we went over the hills to Weimar and on west to spend the night of April 6 in Erfurt.

"There could be danger awaiting us in Erfurt," warned Luther when we took our lunch break. "I went to the university there. However, from what I've heard, the leaders are firmly aligned with the Roman church, so they may be particularly displeased with me. They may feel I have embarrassed them and hurt the reputation of their school. If any problem appears," he said, turning to Casper Sturm, "let's ride right on through. We can camp a night in the woods if need be."

"No one would dare threaten the charge of the imperial herald," said Sturm in disgust.

"No one you could charge or identify," agreed Luther. "But crowds have a mind of their own and can easily turn into an angry mob. I have written to my friend, Lang, in Eisenach. If there is any trouble, he is prepared to come to our rescue and take us secretly on our way."

Sturm snorted his disregard for such arrangements, tossed the chicken bone he had been gnawing on into the brush and stood up. "If there's a chance that we will have to travel beyond Erfurt tonight, let's get going or we'll be traveling in the dark."

But long before our little party reached the gates of Erfurt, we were met by a crowd of joyful students declaring their support for Luther. They escorted us into the city and through the narrow streets right to the university. Far from being an embarrassment, Doctor Luther was considered a hero.

The following morning, Sunday, Luther preached in the university chapel. So many people wanted to hear him that the foundation of the porch cracked from the weight of people waiting to crowd into the church.

In the afternoon we traveled on to Gotha just a few miles down the road. There Luther again preached. It was Palm Sunday, and the crowds had been wild with enthusiasm and support for Luther. I could see that the spirit of the people as well as what Doctor Luther was saying was having an influence on Casper Sturm. The imperial herald always stood at the back with his arms crossed. At first he had been very somber whenever Luther was speaking of the Gospel and the problems in the church, but more and more I noticed Sturm smiling and nodding in agreement.

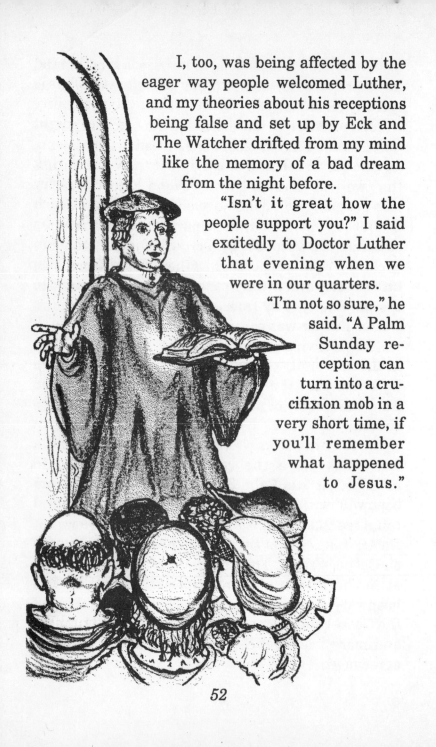

I, too, was being affected by the eager way people welcomed Luther, and my theories about his receptions being false and set up by Eck and The Watcher drifted from my mind like the memory of a bad dream from the night before.

"Isn't it great how the people support you?" I said excitedly to Doctor Luther that evening when we were in our quarters.

"I'm not so sure," he said. "A Palm Sunday reception can turn into a crucifixion mob in a very short time, if you'll remember what happened to Jesus."

Luther stood by the window, hands clasped behind his back, and looked out into Gotha's streets. "This is actually making me more wary than the possibility of highway robbers or the legal tricks that Eck might try to pull before the council."

But as the days passed, Luther did not shrink from the crowds that seemed to be larger in every town through which we passed. And, when at each evening's stop the people begged him to preach, he would go to the church and give them a sermon of an hour or more. But the pace exhausted him, and before we made it over the hills to Eisenach, he came down with a fever. Still the crowds met us in the towns and villages, but Luther could no longer preach in their churches.

The days passed and my master pretty much recovered by the time we arrived at Frankfurt. The next day we crossed the Rhine River and traveled up its broad valley to the town of Oppenheim, from where we could almost see the cathedral towers in Worms. Our journey was almost over.

"Let's get an early start tomorrow," said Luther that evening as we sat around the table in the local inn.

"Suits me," said Sturm. "It's been several weeks since I've seen my family."

"I didn't know you had a family," said Brother Nicholas.

"You never asked," said Sturm. It was true. We knew very little about the imperial herald, probably because we'd never bothered to ask. The whole trip had focused on Doctor Luther, his ideas, his dangers, and the people's response to him.

"I'm sorry," said Luther, looking pained. "I would have made a greater effort to leave Wittenberg sooner had I known. How many children do you have?"

"Three girls and two boys, and I'll be as glad to see them as my wife."

The image of the imperial herald riding into Wittenberg and looking down on the crowd by Raven's Tavern came into my mind. I could hardly imagine little children running to greet him—even his own.

Just as we finished eating we were joined by a stranger, a former monk who introduced himself as Martin Bucer. "I bring a message," he said, "from the great knight, Franz von Sickingen. He admires your fight against Rome. And he is willing to defend you militarily if you wish to take refuge with him."

I immediately realized that such a move on Luther's part—when he had been summoned to court—could be considered treasonous. There were rumors of war among the peasants and even with powerful warlords like Sickingen. But the empire was also held together by religious connections. If Luther sided with Sickingen, it could double their power.

Luther looked over at Casper Sturm. Sturm said, "Excuse me, gentlemen, but I think I'll be turning in. An early start tomorrow?" And with that he left the table, not staying to hear Luther's response one way or the other.

"That," said Luther to Martin Bucer, "is the imperial herald. We all could have been arrested for treason."

Bucer's face turned gray. "I had no idea. I never imagined that the herald would be eating with you. Usually . . ."

"Yes, I know," said Luther. "Usually the nobility do not socialize with the accused. But we have become . . . almost friends."

Suddenly, I saw Casper Sturm in a whole new light. He may have been the imperial herald, but his heart had been touched by Doctor Luther's message and person. He had left the table to protect Luther and to give him the freedom to accept the offer if he wanted to.

"Thank Sickingen for me," said Luther. "Maybe some other time I will need his hospitality. But right now I must go to Worms."

The next morning we were loading the wagon before the sun peeked over the hills on the east side of the Rhine. Still, there were a dozen townspeople who accompanied us out of town and promised that they would be praying for Doctor Luther.

Several miles outside Worms I pulled the wagon to a stop on the top of a hill high enough to see over the valley; at some distance we could see a cloud of dust rising through the trees. Casper Sturm straightened in his saddle and called back to us, "If there's any problem, let me handle it."

When we had driven down off the hill and were traveling among the trees, we discovered the source of dust. It was a crowd of people on horseback and on foot; among them Luther recognized some members of Duke Frederick's court. When the multitude recognized who we were, they ran toward us cheering and clapping.

As I clucked to the nervous horses, I noticed that there were several nobles, a number of other university professors, and at least a hundred horsemen—some of them heavily armed—who had ridden out to welcome us.

"I don't like this," Luther said as we approached the gates of the city.

"Why not?" I asked. I thought it was great.

"It's too much like Christ's triumphal entry into Jerusalem. No good can come of this."

More people joined us as we traveled through the city streets, until at about ten in the morning we came to the house of the Knights of Saint John. There we were informed that Duke Frederick had arranged rooms for us at his own expense.

We were safely at our destination, and a good thing, too. I don't think we could have pushed our way any farther through the streets packed with people.

Doctor Luther stood in the wagon, waving to the people, then climbed down and went with Brother Nicholas into the house. I busied myself carrying in our things.

Finally, when I came out for the last load, the crowd had thinned. But across the street among some other men I saw John Eck. I just stood there looking at him for a couple minutes, then grabbed the last bag and went in.

It was a sober reminder that more than friends were waiting for us in the City of Worms.

Chapter 6

Bound and Gagged

THE VERY NEXT AFTERNOON a marshal knocked at our lodgings and summoned Doctor Luther to the bishop's palace where Emperor Charles had taken up temporary residence. We left immediately with the marshal. I was surprised to see that Casper Sturm accompanied us, as did several other of Luther's supporters.

A crowd packed the street in front of our lodging. More people were on the roofs of the adjoining buildings looking down at us. We tried to make our way through the mass, but it was impossible, so we retreated and went out the back way and down the side streets and alleys.

At the bishop's palace we were taken to a small hall which was packed with spectators. The emperor sat at one end, surrounded by the Imperial Council. I stood gawking at all the splendid nobles, almost forgetting why we were there. Me! In the same room with the emperor! If only my mother could see me now.

Then suddenly the crowd quieted as John Eck

stood up and said, "Most Honorable Doctor Luther, we are so grateful that you could be with us. We trust your journey was pleasant." Right away I was suspicious. His words did not seem sincere. Then he went on and we got the real bite of his attitude: "You are here to answer charges of heresy, and we do not want this hearing to turn into a debate. Therefore, you are instructed to answer only the questions put to you and make no other statements. Is that understood?"

Brother Nicholas and I and some others who openly supported Luther gathered close around Luther. He seemed at ease, smiling and looking around at the crowd that was made up of both his friends and enemies. He wore the clothes of an Augustinian monk, a leather belt over his dark, coarsely spun robe. And in the style of monks, he had freshly shaved the top of his head, leaving a ring of hair above his ears and around the back as though he were naturally bald. Doctor Luther was not yet forty years old, but his stocky body was strong for one who spent most of his time in a classroom.

The tall John Eck was quite a contrast to the short Martin Luther as he stood behind the bench waiting for Luther's commitment to not engage in debate. Finally my master said, "I will answer only as God bids me."

Eck was not pleased. He looked toward the emperor, but the emperor did not respond one way or the other. Finally, Eck proceeded, referring to the pile of books on the bench in front of him. "Martin Luther, His Imperial Majesty has summoned you for two reasons: to know whether you acknowledge having written these books; and having written them, whether you are willing to renounce them. What do you say?"

Then a secretary read the names of the books piled on the bench.

Luther said, "Yes, I wrote those books, if they are indeed the titles mentioned. As to whether I can renounce their content, that would take some discussion, and you do not want any debate."

"Why must there be discussion?" challenged Eck.

"First of all, no one in this room would argue against the majority of their content. To deny that material would in itself be heresy since we all can agree that it is from the Holy Scriptures. As for the other content, the material which you and the church of Rome might object to, I cannot deny anything unless it is shown to me to be in conflict with the Scriptures. After all, it was Jesus himself who said, 'Whoever denies me before men, him will I deny before my Father in heaven.' I would at least like time to consider these matters."

It was a fine opening, I thought. But although Luther had spoken boldly, he seemed to be very nervous. Of course we all had reason to be nervous, standing there in the presence of the emperor and the other nobles. For the first time I began to wish I had taken my mother's advice and stayed in Duben, because Eck came back just as strongly on the attack.

"What do you mean, you need time? Have you not had time enough ever since you were summoned to

this court? Maybe, instead of violating the pope's bull and preaching in every village as you traveled here, you should have been preparing to answer His Imperial Majesty. Do you not respect this court and the *emperor's* valuable time?"

"Of course I respect the emperor and this court. It's just that these are weighty matters, and I would not want to do harm to God's Word or my own soul by denying something that is, in fact, true."

After that, things started to go badly. Others stood and protested that Luther should not be given any further time to prepare his case. The evening wore on and lights in the hall were lit. Soon food and drink were brought for the emperor and other nobles behind the bench, but no provision was made for Doctor Luther or the rest of us. I began to worry that in his weakened condition after his recent illness,

Doctor Luther could be in great need of nourishment. I knew I was getting hungry.

Finally, I slipped out of the crowded room thinking that I would get something for us to eat and drink. It was dark outside in the open portal that ran up the side of the hall, and I stood there thinking of where I could go to get some provisions. Suddenly, a figure stepped up beside me. As my eyes adjusted to the darkness, I realized it was The Watcher.

I jumped as though she were death itself when the girl reached out and touched me. "Come with me," she said, allowing the long scarf she held over her nose and mouth to fall away from her hauntingly beautiful face. Her blue eyes flashed as she said, "We must talk!"

The mystery of the girl almost caused me to follow, but I had more sense than that. "Who are you, anyway? And why are you always following us?" I asked. She looked around as though hoping no one heard, but I continued just as loudly, "I know why you follow us. It's Doctor Luther, isn't it?"

"Yes," she hissed. "Now you must come with me."

"Not on my life. I will never betray him."

Just then a group of people came out of the hall and turned our way. The Watcher quickly adjusted the scarf over her face again, turned, and hurried away.

That was a close one. But now I had my proof. She *had* been following us all the way to Worms, and her interest was Luther. She had said so herself. This time when I told the others, they would have to believe me. I started to go back into the court but realized there was no way I could say anything about her during the hearing. My report would have to wait until we were alone later that night. So I went on out to the street to find some food and drink, all the while keeping a sharp eye out for The Watcher.

I had not walked far from the bishop's palace when two figures jumped out from a narrow passageway between two buildings and grabbed me. Before I knew what was happening they pulled me into the passageway and tied a rag around my mouth to gag me. But then I began fighting as hard as I could. I stomped on one's foot and tried to knee the other. With all my strength I twisted and turned to free my arms, but there were two of them, and soon they overcame me and had my arms bound behind my back.

"Just calm down," said a man's voice. "We intend

you no harm. We just need to talk to you."

Right. I'd already heard that one tonight. But this time there didn't seem to be much I could do without getting myself hurt, so I decided to go along, looking every moment for some means of escape. I hoped they would take me out into the street where we might meet other people. Then I'd make a run for it, trusting that they wouldn't risk hitting me over the head or something worse right in front of others.

But my hopes were in vain. They kept to the dark passageways and corridors of the old city. Then they pushed me through a door and—nearly carrying me by each shoulder—marched me down two flights of steps to a damp and dark dungeon. It was lit by a single flickering candle, and the bulk of a third stranger was seated behind a small table. The huge door clanged closed behind me.

I looked around at my surroundings. If this wasn't a prison that I'd landed in, it was the next thing to it.

Chapter 7

The Assignment

THE ROOM WAS DAMP AND COLD, and the single candle cast flickering shadows on the stone walls. There were no windows in the cell.

"What's your name, lad?" asked the large man behind the small table. He nodded at my captors and they removed the gag.

"Karl."

"Well, Master Karl, do you have a last name?"

"Schumacher. My name is Karl Schumacher. But why did you bring me here? Why are my hands tied? Let me go."

"Please forgive us," said the man behind the table. He was large and rugged looking but not unkind in his appearance. "I hope these men did not hurt you, but it seems you would not join us by simple invitation. We needed to talk to you immediately. We could not risk missing our opportunity."

"So you jumped me in a dark alley, tied me up, and dragged me down here to this dungeon. Why? I haven't done anything wrong." I hoped they could not hear the wild thumping of my heart.

"Of course not." He looked at the two men who were standing on each side of me. "Gentlemen, let's untie Karl. I'm sure he no longer needs to be restrained."

The man on my right untied the thong around my wrists. I rubbed them to get the feeling back into my hands. "Thank you," I managed. "Now why did you bring me here? I want to go."

"We need your help with Doctor Luther."

My mind was spinning. I had once heard that if you are ever captured, the best time to make your escape is immediately. Well, it seemed that I was already too late for that. They had me in a stone cell behind a closed door. But maybe I could talk my way out of this prison. I'd have to be careful, though—not give away anything that would betray Doctor Luther.

"I'll not answer any questions as long as you have me locked in this prison."

"Prison?" said the large man, and the other two chuckled. "Karl, you're not in prison. We just needed somewhere to talk in private."

"Then how come that big door is bolted behind me?"

"It's not bolted. Franz, show Karl that he's not locked in here. Leave the door open a little bit if that makes him more comfortable."

Franz, the man on my right, opened the door a few inches.

"Does that mean I can walk out of here?" I turned and started for the door, wanting to seize my first opportunity, thinking it might be my last.

"Wait a minute," said Franz, putting his hand on my shoulder as he stepped between me and the door.

Just as I thought, it wasn't going to be that easy.

"Give us a minute," said the large man.

"It looks like I have no choice," I said.

"We just want to talk to you about Doctor Luther. We need your help. Look, Karl," continued the large man, "we represent a very important person. You might be able to guess who he is, but we cannot say his name." (Yes, well, I *did* have my ideas who was behind this—probably Eck.) "Our master wishes to make sure Luther is treated fairly, and that's why we need your help."

"I will never betray Doctor Luther no matter how long you keep me in this dungeon."

"Good," said the large man. "We need loyalty. But we have no intention of keeping you down here. If the trial for Luther goes badly, we may need to arrange his escape. But to do so, we'll need an insider. And that's where you come in. We want you to tell us about his every move before he makes it so that he can be rescued if need be."

Suddenly I began to feel very confused. Here these fellows had jumped me and thrown me in prison—or at least it seemed like a prison to me. But they claimed it was not a prison, that I was free to go. On the other hand, they insisted on talking to me first. Worse still, it sounded like they wanted me to spy on Doctor Luther. But then they were talking about rescuing him, arranging his "escape." What was going on? What did it all mean?

"Karl, if John Eck has his way, your master will be condemned as a heretic. If that happens, it is very hard to predict what the emperor will do. If it strikes his fancy, he might dismiss the whole thing. On the other hand, he could as easily condemn Luther to be burned at the stake. We have no way of knowing."

"Therefore," Franz spoke up, "if we are to save Luther we must be ready to move at a moment's notice. So we need your help."

Who were these people? I had at first been sure they were Eck's representatives. But possibly they were Duke Frederick's men. How could I be sure?

"Who are you?" I demanded.

"Who we are—personally—doesn't make any difference, Karl. Will you help us? Will you help Luther?"

"But if you won't tell me who you are, at least tell me who you work for."

"As I said earlier, we can't say our master's name. You can probably guess, but if you were ever questioned, it would be in everyone's best interest if you could honestly answer that his name was never mentioned. Do you understand?"

Well, I did, in a way. And then again I didn't! I needed time to think, time to figure out whether these men were setting a trap or planning to help Luther. "What do you want from me?" I asked, hoping that a little more information would help me figure things out.

"You'll be our inside man. It will be your duty to know where Luther is going and when—every minute of the day or night. Things could go badly for him at any point. We can't take time to chase him down if he's taken it into his mind to go speak in some chapel. If he is condemned, we may have no more than a couple of hours to get him out of town. We will remain in regular contact with you so that you can tell us where he will be."

"Is that all?" I asked, thinking it was far too much if these were enemies. But the plan did sound reasonable—the kind of plan friends would make.

"Yes, that's all—be our insider and keep us informed, and help out when the time comes."

"When what time comes?"

"If we need to rescue him."

"Can I think about it?" I asked.

The large man glanced at the two men at my side. "Tomorrow. We need your answer by tomorrow at the latest. If you won't help, we'll have to get someone else. But you are the ideal insider. You have been with him from Wittenberg. As a boy, as his servant, you can come and go without anyone noticing. We need you. Your master, Doctor Luther needs you. Don't let him down!"

"Can I go now?"

"Yes. Our contact will approach you tomorrow while you are at court. There will be a password. The contact will say, 'I rode through Duben.' Give your answer to that person only. Speak to no one else about this. Now go."

I turned and left, stumbling up the stone steps in the dark. "I rode through Duben." What a strange password. A lot of people ride through Duben. That's my home town, and I had ridden through just a few days before. Did he know where I came from? It seemed very eerie to have someone know more about me than I knew about him.

The next day other court business delayed Doctor Luther's hearing until late in the afternoon. For me it was very hard to wait, but Luther used the time peacefully, preparing what he was going to say.

An old friend of Luther's, a monk named Brother John Petzensteiner, joined us for lunch. "I have come to join you," he said to Luther. "Whatever your lot may be, that will be my lot."

"That's a rather bold claim," laughed Luther. "Maybe your name should be Brother Peter—your claim sounds something like Peter's boast to Christ our Master."

Brother John was obviously hurt, though I don't think Doctor Luther had any intention of scolding him. Soon, however, the tension eased, and they were discussing old times together. Luther insisted that Brother John stay with us in our rooms, small as they were.

When we were finally called for the hearing, it was to a much larger hall in the bishop's palace, but it was just as crowded. In fact, even the emperor had a hard time getting through the mass of people to his place.

When the hearing got underway, John Eck started right in by demanding that Luther answer the second question of the day before: was he ready to renounce the content of his writings?

Doctor Luther spoke boldly, his preparation of the day and the help of the Lord giving him extra strength. Luther used many verses from the Bible to prove the rightness of his claims and objections to the corruption in the Roman church.

When he finished, Eck said tersely, "Heresy. All of it is heresy!"

Martin Luther turned to the emperor and said, "Your Majesty, unless I am shown from the Scriptures that I have made mistakes, I am neither able nor willing to revoke even one word of what I have written. Here I stand; God help me, I cannot do otherwise."

I thought it was a wonderful conclusion as did

most of his other German friends who were standing with us. The hearing was then dismissed, and we were all congratulating each other as we pushed our way out through the crowd. When we got outside, some of the crowd was cheering . . . but then swelling louder and louder rose another sound, a large number of people chanting: "To the flames! To the flames!

To the flames!" Fear tightened my throat. In my mind I saw the ladder with the "heretic" tipping over into the flames five years ago. A chill went through me. The emperor had not yet made his judgment, and it could be death.

Then, as I strained against the crowd to see ahead through the night, I heard a female voice next to me saying, "I rode through Duben. I rode through Duben."

I whipped around, and there was The Watcher tugging on my sleeve.

Chapter 8

The Flight of the Condemned

"COME ON. COME ON. I need to talk to you," The Watcher said as she pulled me to the edge of the crowd.

"You? You're my contact?" I blurted.

"Quiet," she said, but the mob was so noisy that only those closest to us could have heard either of us. She kept pulling on my arm, and soon we turned in through a gate to the secluded plaza of a fine villa.

"So that was you who rode through Duben the other night. What were you doing snooping in our wagon?"

"Nothing. I just wanted to make sure it was yours—that you were staying there."

"Why did you want to know that? Why were you following us?"

"There's no time to explain all that now. Have you made up your mind to help us . . . or not?"

"How should I know? I don't even know who you people are."

"What difference does it make? We're friends of Luther, and he may need our help. Didn't you hear what the crowd was chanting just now? There are many who want him burned at the stake."

I tried to swallow, but my throat still felt tight and dry. I could still hear the chants in the street. "I know that. And you and those men who ambushed me last night might be part of them." I stared at her, getting a good look at her face for the first time. "At least tell me your name."

"My name is Arlene . . ."

Just then a group of people came through the gate. They must have lived in the villa because they immediately started yelling at us: "You there. This is a private courtyard. How did you get in here? Get out! Get out, now!"

The Watcher ducked her head and in a moment we were back on the street, which was still filled with people. "Make up your mind—soon! Remember your assignment," she hissed. Then The Watcher slipped into the crowd and was gone.

I made my way back to our quarters, thinking all the way about what I should do. Finally I decided I needed to talk to Doctor Luther and tell him that I had met The Watcher, that her name was Arlene, but Arlene . . . what?

However, when I got back to our rooms there was a celebration going on. Along with Brother Nicholas and Brother John, many strangers were there congratulating Luther on his brilliant defense or advising him on what next steps he should take. Luther greeted everyone by raising both fists above his head and declaring, "I've come through; I've come through." He felt certain that tomorrow he would receive a favorable ruling.

But early the next morning when two guards arrived at our door, I wasn't so sure. Had they come to take Doctor Luther to prison? No. I soon discovered that they had been sent merely to escort him through the crowd back to the palace hall.

Our mood was very confident.

When the council was gathered once more, Emperor Charles rose to speak. This in itself was quite a surprise. No one expected him to respond to Luther directly. He was young and weak-hearted and let his advisers establish policy—at least that's what we had been told. But there he was reading his judgment.

". . . in view of the State's long tradition of supporting the church, I, too, will support the church. I cannot accept that one man's opinion is correct if all the church leaders and theologians speak against him.

"I should have moved against this Martin Luther's heretical ideas much earlier. I intend to send him safely back to Wittenberg, but only because I keep my promises of safe conduct. But no more preaching. No more teaching. If he wants continued safety he must remain silent. All of his books and writings are to be burned. Anyone caught reading, printing, or distributing them should be condemned.

"Once he has arrived home, my promise of safe conduct will have ended, and I will proceed against him as a notorious heretic."

I was stunned. I couldn't believe what I was

hearing. But Charles wasn't through.

Turning to the rest of the council members, he said, "I call upon each one of you to prove your loyalty to the empire by doing your duty and keeping your promise to me. I agreed to hear this man fairly. And you," he said as he looked directly at Duke Frederick, "agreed to uphold the Imperial ruling."

The whole court erupted with shouts—some in support of the emperor, some in protest. And then in the middle of the hubbub I noticed Duke Frederick rise from his seat and slip out.

I guess no one had expected such a strong statement from the emperor. And no one with any real authority rose to defend Doctor Luther. There was just a lot of grumbling and shouting. Soon Luther and the rest of our party were ushered out of the hall as the Imperial Council moved on to discuss other matters of state.

That evening some other friends came to our room to discuss Doctor Luther's plight with him and Brothers Nicholas and John. There was no certainty that Luther would be sentenced to death, but the possibility was greater than ever. Some of the Council members who favored Luther were trying to arrange further hearings on Luther's behalf. Maybe, they hoped, the emperor's declaration could be softened.

Days passed as negotiations continued. Sometimes Luther was summoned to testify before various committees, but no real improvement happened. At least once a day I saw The Watcher—or Arlene, as

I now knew her. I would be walking to one of the meetings with Doctor Luther, or coming back from shopping at the market, or delivering a message, and there she'd be standing in a doorway or by a fountain or reading the daily news posters on the bulletin boards. Each time I would just shake my head. I had pretty much decided to trust her and the men behind her, but there was still some doubt, and I didn't want to commit myself. Besides, there was no news to report.

Then one day Casper Sturm, the imperial herald, came to our quarters. "There are only twenty-two days remaining on your guarantee of safe conduct," he said very solemnly to Doctor Luther. "I think it might be wise if you did not wait too long."

"But certainly it does not take that long to get back to Wittenberg," said Brother Nicholas, who was trying to mend his sandal.

"No. It is quite easy to make the trip in a couple of weeks or less," Sturm agreed, "but it would also be possible for bad weather or illness to delay you so you would be on the road past your safe-conduct period. Then you could be in greater danger."

"I was sick on our trip down here," said Luther, "and it did not slow us much. And how could bad weather do anything worse than make our traveling unpleasant?"

"I have seen heavy thunderstorms flood streams and rivers so that they were impassible for two or three days at a time in the spring," said the herald. "But to be frank with you, Doctor Luther, the greatest danger is from your enemies who might *arrange* delays—a broken wagon wheel, lame horses, bandits—many things can go wrong on the highway. You must realize, Doctor Luther, now that you have been condemned by the emperor, your life could be easily taken by others. Your remaining time of safe conduct may protect you from official harm, but others . . . they could attack you without fear of prosecution. You are a condemned man."

"Hmmm, yes. I see what you mean," said Luther.

Brother John spoke up. "You know, Doctor Luther, I don't think there's much value in remaining in Worms any longer. I've gone to a couple of those meetings with you, and I don't think anything is being accomplished."

"I suppose you're right," said Luther. "I might as well get back to my students at the university."

"There'll be no imperial escort for you on this trip," said the herald, "but I wish you well. I've come to respect your fight, Doctor Luther."

"Thank you," said Luther. The two men clasped hands briefly.

"Let's leave tomorrow," said Luther as soon as the herald had taken his leave. "If we have no imperial escort, maybe we can slip out of the city unnoticed. A quiet trip home could be the safest."

"I agree," said Brother Nicholas. "But your departure will be known within the day. People are always coming by and asking to see you."

"That's true." Luther looked out the window, rubbing his chin. "What we need is for one of you brothers to stay behind for a few days. If you could simply tell people that I am not available, my absence wouldn't be so apparent."

"I'll be glad to do that," offered Brother Nicholas. "Since I arrived with you, most people will assume we would leave together."

"Good. Brother John, can you come with us?"

"I told you I was with you all the way."

"Then why don't you two brothers begin packing. I'm going out into the streets and talk to people so that many get a good chance to see me. That should hold them for a while."

"Don't go preaching, now," said Brother Nicholas. "You must not tempt the emperor to enforce his ban on your public speaking."

"I'll be careful. And Karl, why don't you go purchase supplies and get our wagon and horses prepared. No one will take much notice of you. Let's plan to leave as quietly as possible tomorrow."

All the rest of that afternoon I made trips to the market. I bought bread and cheese and apples and jugs of wine, each time trying not to carry so much as to attract attention. Then in the evening I made similar trips to the stable to load things into the wagon, waiting half an hour or an hour between each one so as not to attract attention.

It was late when I made my last trip to the stable—without a lantern—but I decided to give the horses extra feed in preparation for the journey. I scooped oats into the feed bins of the first two horses, then groped in the dark of the last stall. As I felt my

way along the horse's flank, I
stumbled over something in the
straw on the floor. As I fell,
I suddenly found myself
tangled with an-
other body.
And then
someone
screamed.

"What's going on out there," called the stable man
from his shack in front of the barn.

Before I could answer, someone clamped a strong
hand over my mouth. "It's me, Arlene," said The
Watcher's hushed voice. "I didn't mean to scream,
but you stepped on me." And then the hand was
removed from my mouth.

"What . . ?" I started to protest.

"Shhh. Just answer the man."

"Nothing," I called. "I just tripped over something."

A door slammed.

"What are you doing here?" I asked.

"You're getting ready to leave, aren't you?" said Arlene.

"What makes you think so?"

"I've been watching you all day—going to market, packing the wagon. I figured you'd check your horses, but I fell asleep waiting. Now, when are you leaving?"

Before I realized what I was doing, I told Arlene our whole plan. I hadn't really decided to trust her, but there—I'd gone ahead and done it.

"I think it's wise," she said. "I just hope you can get out of town without being noticed." And then in the dark she laid her hand on my arm. "Thank you, Karl, for trusting me. You did the right thing."

"How'd you know my name?"

"It's only fair. I told you mine, didn't I?"

"Yes, but I *didn't* tell you mine."

"Well, someone else did. Goodnight, Karl." And then she was gone into the dark.

When I got back to our rooms I was tired and went right to bed, but Arlene filled my dreams, riding off into a moonlit night with her long dark hair flowing behind her.

We'd hoped to leave early the next morning, but Doctor Luther was summoned to a meeting that did not finish until after ten o'clock, so it was nearly lunch before I pulled the wagon around and Doctor Luther and Brother John climbed in.

We rattled down the street as though we were in no particular hurry and turned toward the city gate. All seemed well. No one seemed to be noticing our departure.

But as soon as we passed through the gate, we were greeted by a small troop of horsemen. There must have been at least twenty of them, many of them armed.

"We're your escort," announced a man with a pointed gray beard and a brass helmet.

How had they known?

Chapter 9

Escape Down the Werra

THE HORSEMEN RODE IN FRONT, alongside, and behind us. I barely had to drive our horses; they
just plodded along as part of the herd. Had it been
Arlene who had arranged the escort, I wondered,
holding the reins idly. There was no slipping out of
the city unnoticed now. Soon everyone would know.
Why had I trusted her? It had been foolish of me to
let down my guard.

But Doctor Luther and Brother John didn't seem
concerned about our company and traveled along in
high spirits until we reached the town of Oppenheim
late that afternoon. Frequently Luther would get out
his lute and lead everyone in a country folk song.
Sometimes he would put new, Christian words to it.
We took a break in the marketplace, where the people
greeted Luther. Suddenly, we were startled by a
horseman who came riding at full gallop and reined
hard to a stop among the people in the marketplace.

When the cloud of dust settled, we saw it was
Casper Sturm, the imperial herald!

"I thought you couldn't accompany us!" said Luther.

"And I'm not here," laughed Sturm as he swung down from his lathered horse. "At least I'm not here *officially*—not as the imperial herald, that is. But no one else need know that. Actually, the emperor gave me a holiday from my service, so I decided to tag along for a couple of days."

I was glad to see him. He'd become a friend we could depend on in situations where I trusted very few.

Before setting up camp for the night we crossed the Rhine River, and most of our escort turned back instead of paying the toll. Maybe they considered the imperial herald's presence sufficient security; maybe they had to get back to families and other business; or maybe—I speculated—maybe some of them were not along to protect us after all. Maybe they intended some harm that was blocked by Sturm's arrival. Whatever the case, from there on we were accompanied by a small escort of only four other men plus Casper Sturm.

Our journey was uneventful for the next three days except for Luther's insistence on preaching in every town where he was invited. We warned him against this, reminding him that preaching was in direct defiance of the emperor's orders, but Luther persisted.

Then one day after a rather strong protest from the imperial herald, Luther said, "I have not accepted the emperor's condemnation any more than I accepted the pope's bull against me. God is my judge! Why should I obey man rather than God?"

"But my Dear Doctor," protested Casper Sturm, "if you will not take care for your own safety, consider the rest of us. Can you not see how your preaching compromises my presence with you? I do no wrong in merely accompanying you. I am on holiday, and you are still under the emperor's safe passage. But to expect me to stand by while you defy the emperor . . . well, it makes me equally guilty."

"I am truly sorry," said Luther, softening in his way of speaking. "However, the Scriptures say: 'Preach the word; be instant in season, out of season; reprove, rebuke, exhort with all longsuffering and doctrine.' The emperor may have declared my preaching 'out of season,' but that does not release me from the obligation to declare God's Word anyway."

We stood about in awkward silence as the disagreement between Luther and Sturm came to a deadlock.

Finally Sturm bowed his head and then looked up at Luther. "Maybe I should turn back. I only have a day or two left, anyway, before I would have to return to court. You don't seem to be encountering any danger. You have friends in each town who will be looking out for your safety."

"Maybe that would be best," said Luther. "I understand your situation. We greatly appreciate your service and . . ." slowly Luther extended his hand, ". . . your friendship." The imperial herald took the offered hand and clasped it warmly.

"Maybe it would be best if the rest of us left you at this point, too, Doctor Luther," said one of the armed men who had been accompanying us from Worms.

I was shocked. We had never expected an escort, but then our plan had been to travel unnoticed. Now we had been traveling four days with a large group. People all along our route knew we were coming, almost like it had been when we were going to Worms. Without Casper Sturm and the others in our escort, we would be completely vulnerable. I squinted my eyes and looked at the mountains which had been creeping closer, where the forests were thicker and the towns more remote. But what could we do?

That evening Doctor Luther preached in the town square in Hersfeld. The people were begging him to speak, but the local priest would not risk offering the chapel, though he kept claiming he greatly admired Doctor Luther. So everyone gathered in the square and lit the place with torches held high on poles.

I was standing in the shadows at the edge of the crowd when a voice said to me, "I see you have lost your escort." By now the voice was familiar. I turned and could just make out in the darkness the figure of The Watcher.

"Arlene! What are you doing here?"

"Shhh. I'm your contact; remember?"

"But I had no idea you would follow us from Worms."

"Well, I did."

Her beauty was magnified in the flickering light of the torches, but I could not erase all my suspicion. "You know you ruined our quiet departure from Worms, don't you? That was really stupid arranging for a troop of twenty horsemen to escort us."

"Me? We didn't arrange for an escort."

"Well, who else knew? I trusted you and told you we were leaving. Otherwise we planned to leave secretly. No one else knew."

"When you spend all day shopping and loading your wagon, several people might know—the stable man for one."

I had never thought of him. After leaving Worms I had assumed it was Arlene and the men behind her who had arranged the escort. Though it shook my trust in her, I had finally accepted the escort as a safety measure.

"We were actually worried about the escort ourselves," said Arlene, "especially when the imperial herald joined you. It looked like a trap."

"How'd you know Casper Sturm joined us? Have you been spying on us all the way?"

"It's my *job* to be your contact. So I have to stay close enough to make contact when need be."

"Well, you needn't worry about Casper Sturm. He's become a loyal friend, as loyal as they come. I'd trust him before I'd trust . . ." I was going to say "you," but as I looked into the deep blue of her eyes in the torchlight, it didn't seem like the right thing to say.

"I'll see you again at Eisenach," she said and started to leave.

"Wait!" I said. "We're not going on to Eisenach. Doctor Luther wants to turn east before we get there and head up into the Thuringer Mountains. He has some relatives there he wants to visit."

"Where, exactly?" Arlene asked.

"I don't know. He mentioned a village named 'Mohra,' or something."

"Thank you. We will meet again." And then she was gone.

The next morning we got a very early start and I found myself looking for Arlene at every crossroads and in every little village we passed through. I blamed my daydreams on the boredom of driving that old wagon mile after mile. Certainly *I* wouldn't be thinking about some girl if there'd been anything more interesting to do.

We turned east on a smaller road and soon began ascending the mountains. "It's actually a shortcut," said Luther. "Instead of going on north to Eisenach before we turn east, we're taking a cutoff and will catch the main road at Gotha. We'll miss Eisenach completely."

"Well, if it's a shortcut, why doesn't everyone take it?" I asked.

"You'll see," said Luther.

And in a short time I did. The road was so steep

that we were slowed down considerably. Again and again as we crept along my mind would drift to Arlene: bumping into her outside Raven's Tavern back in Wittenberg, Arlene racing through Duben in the middle of the night with her hair flying behind her, Arlene looking so beautiful in the soft torchlight the last time I'd seen her.

If I could really trust her, I thought, guiding the horses around a place where the heavy spring rains had washed out part of the road, she *was* the kind of girl a fellow could get interested in. There was no denying her haunting beauty. But there was more. What courage she must have to be out on the highway by herself! She had confidence, a self-assurance I didn't see much in other girls I knew. And if she really supported Luther's teachings . . . that spoke well of her faith in God.

On the other hand, I snorted to myself, she must not be from a very good family if her parents let her travel around the country alone like that. It just wasn't done!

In spite of the rough road, Doctor Luther was sitting in the back of the wagon, sometimes working on a sermon, sometimes playing on his lute and singing. Brother John was curled up among our bags . . . asleep again, as usual.

We reached the summit, and I guided our wagon down the steep road to the ferry that crossed the Werra River. The river at that point is calm, but as I came down the mountain I could see that just a little farther downstream the river became a wild and rushing torrent cutting through a steep gorge.

This was a better ferry than the one we rode on over the Elbe River outside Wittenberg, and there was no problem loading the wagon and our three horses. I blocked our wheels, paid the ferryman, and settled back to enjoy viewing the rich forest that clung to the sheer walls of the river's gorge. I noticed that these woods had dark evergreens among them, offsetting the light green growth of new spring leaves on the hardwood trees.

We were in the middle of the river when I saw a group of men waiting on the opposite bank. They were all mounted on strong horses that pawed the ferry landing impatiently. The men were heavily armed, some with the armor of knights, but they carried no flag or banner to announce what lord they rode for.

A chill ran through me, and I jumped down from the wagon. "Do you know who those men are?" I asked the ferryman as he pulled steadily on his come-along and drew us across the river.

He looked up without interrupting his slow pace and squinted across the water. "Can't say as I do. Are you expecting someone to meet you? There are too many of them to ride this ferry in one trip."

Expecting someone? No, we certainly weren't expecting anyone—at least not anyone we wanted to meet. But they might be waiting for us, nonetheless. I mulled over the possibilities. It would make an ideal trap. We couldn't outrun them. In fact, I wouldn't even be able to drive the wagon through the middle of them. And there'd be no hiding from them. We couldn't jump off and run through the brush. There was absolutely no escape.

And then I thought of one.

I scampered around to the back of our wagon and pulled out the old axe that we used to cut firewood when we camped. With one mighty swing I chopped in two the ferry rope that slid across the deck between the guides. It was the rope that was stretched across the whole river and prevented us from floating downstream. It was the same rope that the ferryman was pulling on with his come-along to bring us to the other side.

"Wha—! What have you done?" he screamed as the rope slid instantly through his come-along and splashed into the water at the side of the raft. We were already starting to float downstream.

His yell awoke Brother John and brought Doctor Luther to attention. "What's happening?" asked Luther.

"Those men," I answered, pointing to the river bank. At that very moment they were backing their horses off the landing and guiding them downstream and pointing toward us. "It's an ambush!" I said. "They were waiting for us, and there was no other way to escape."

The current pulled the rope out of the ferryman's hands, and we floated freely toward the narrowing gorge. The ferryman was yelling at me. "You foolish kid. You've lost my ferry, and maybe our lives. Even if we survive the rapids, it will take me weeks to build a new ferry. Are you out of your mind? What possessed you?"

But soon there was no more time for yelling. White water was coming up as we approached the rapids in the gorge. The ferryman ordered Brother John to help him with one oar and Doctor Luther and me to man the other oar. "Watch ahead! Watch ahead!" he yelled. "Just try to keep it off the rocks or it will break up."

We were already starting to bob as we went over the smaller rapids. But ahead I could see much larger ones. Soon he was shouting and pointing for us to guide the ferry back toward the side of the river we'd first started from. Then I could see why. We were headed directly for a waterfall. It was small but big enough to tip us off even if it didn't break up the ferry. Doctor Luther and I pulled for all we were worth on the oar, but it didn't seem like we were making any progress at guiding the ferry. And then slowly we caught a new current that began to spin us sideways but also toward the safer side of the river.

I was actually going backward down the river as we passed the falls. Most of the ferry rode the smooth water, but the end with the ferryman and Brother John went partially over the falls. That twisted the ferry so that it groaned and creaked and snapped loudly enough to be heard over the rush of the river. We all nearly lost our balance, and would probably have fallen to the deck if we hadn't been hanging on to the oars.

The two horses at the front of the wagon remained steady, but the one at the back panicked and began rearing up. On the second time it slipped and fell over the side of the ferry into the river. But it was still firmly tied to the back of the wagon. That halter and rope must have been one of the strongest made because they were pulling the wagon sideways toward the edge of the ferry at the same time they were pulling the horse's head under water.

"Cut him free," yelled Luther as I ran to help. "Cut him free, or we'll lose everything."

I grabbed the axe that was still lying on the deck and hacked the rope in two. The horse quickly swam away even as we floated on downstream, and as I watched, it gained solid ground and scrambled up the bank.

We, however, were still in danger. More white water loomed ahead. And as I glanced at the far shore, I could see the horsemen picking their way along the steep bank in an attempt to keep up with us.

The next stretch of white water included a series of waves higher than the ferry. The ferryman yelled for us to turn the ferry sideways. "We have to roll with these waves, or we'll break apart," he called. Again, we pulled and pulled on our oar and managed to get the ferry almost sideways just as we hit this new stretch of white water.

We bobbed and rolled, all right. Up and down, up and down, up and down. Both remaining horses were driven to their knees and then onto their sides by the rolling of the deck. Their eyes were rolled back and they were squealing like stuck pigs as they tried to regain their feet.

But then we were through and still afloat.

For the next half mile the water was smooth, and I looked back at our pursuers. They had been stopped by the sheer cliffs at the river's bank. There had been no trail by which they could follow us downstream.

We twisted and turned with the river through its narrow gorge and passed over two more stretches of white water—neither as bad as the one that had put the horses down. Then we came out into a small valley where the river ran calmly and were able to slowly guide the ferry to the bank where we managed to beach it on a sandy bar.

Chapter 10

Seized on the Highway

I GUESS THE FERRYMAN was as glad to be alive as we were because he didn't immediately begin yelling at me. Instead, he joined us in getting the wagon off the ferry and onto solid ground. And that wasn't so easy.

First we had to cut some driftwood logs to make a little ramp from the ferry deck down to the sand about two feet below. But then the sand was so soft that the wagon sank nearly to its axles and the horses churned up a mire.

With poles for levers and brush to get some footing on, we finally made it up into a beautiful meadow.

"Now where?" said Brother John.

"This is a fine time to ask that question," growled the ferryman. "You should have thought of that before your fool kid cut us loose. You will pay. You will pay for a new ferry," he said. Then turning to me: "Whatever possessed you to do that?"

"It was those men on the far bank," I said. "They were after us, and there was no other way to escape."

"After you? You're imagining things. What would

they want with an old wagon, a couple of monks, and a crazy kid?"

I looked at Doctor Luther for support, but he just gazed at the afternoon sky. I think he was enjoying the tongue-lashing I was getting.

"Well," I said defensively, "you did see them take off down the river trying to keep up with us, didn't you?"

"I didn't notice." His tone was sarcastic. "But did you ever think that maybe they were trying to help us? We were in considerable danger, in case *you* didn't notice."

"We do have reason to be cautious," said Luther, finally coming to my defense. "There are those who would be glad to see me dead. So we have been on the watch against an attack."

The ferryman looked my master up and down. "You look harmless enough. Why should you have enemies?"

Luther looked at Brother John and then at me. "Does the name Martin Luther mean anything to you?" he asked.

"Martin Luther? Are you Martin Luther? Of course I know about Martin Luther." The man grabbed his hat off his head. "My, oh my. Wait until I tell my wife. What a privilege to have carried you on my ferry."

Luther roared with laughter. "Even after we lost it for you?"

"Don't worry about that. I would have done anything to help you escape," said the ferryman,

twisting his hat in his hands. "And we'll be sure to pay you for the loss of your ferry," reassured Luther.

"Come to think of it, that was pretty smart, kid. What made you think of going down river?"

I shrugged. "There was no place else to go."

"But now the question is, how do we get out of this valley?" put in Brother John.

"Oh, that's no problem," the man said. "We're only about three miles down river from the crossing, and at the end of this valley is a farm. And if it hasn't been washed out with the rains, there's a road from that farm over the mountains to the village of Mohra."

"Mohra?" said Luther. "That's where we were headed. All my relatives live there. Ah-ha! Now I know where we are."

It took us the rest of the afternoon to drive through the dense forest to reach the village of Mohra. The area was very remote. We saw only one woodcutter and two farmers. By dusk we pulled into the little

98

village of Mohra and stopped at a fine house.

"My grandmother lives here," said Luther grinning broadly, and indeed she did. In minutes we were surrounded by more aunts and uncles and cousins than I could count, let alone remember their names.

As though they had been expecting us, Luther's relatives had soon arranged a village potluck in the family garden, and everyone was begging the Doctor to give them a sermon. Of course, he had one ready—the one he had been working on that morning before all the excitement broke loose.

That night I slept well, maybe better than I had on the whole trip. Doctor Luther's grandmother put me up in a room all my own with a feather bed. What luxury!

The next morning we had a truly proper breakfast: fresh milk, fresh bread—so light and soft—with cheese and jam, and tea. Doctor Luther seemed in no hurry to go, either. In fact, every little while some other relative of his would arrive. Many were miners like his father, some were farmers, and others were woodsmen.

It was afternoon before we finally climbed into the wagon loaded with a huge food basket and headed off down the road toward Gotha. I still hadn't seen Arlene, but as I began to think about that incident on the Werra River, my doubts returned. Had she arranged for those men to be waiting for us? If it wasn't her, who had notified them of our approach? The average person would have assumed we would have gone on ahead to Eisenach.

My feelings and thoughts tugged back and forth, not knowing if this was a girl I could trust or not . . . but still *wanting* to trust her.

Finally, I shook my head as if to dismiss her, concluding that we would be in Wittenberg again within a few days. If she showed up there, maybe I could find out what had happened and how she fit into the picture.

Traveling through the dense forest was slower than we had expected. The road was rough and wove in and out of many trees. It was getting on toward sundown and we still had not sighted Gotha.

The road came out of the woods and went along the edge, with the forest on our left side and a beautiful meadow on our right. Across the meadow was a small peasant village. There were only four or five poor hovels in which people lived, but since dark was approaching, I asked, "Do you think we should spend the night over there? Or should we look for a place to camp on our own?"

Luther and Brother John studied the shacks, trying to decide if the people were too poor to take in three more hungry mouths. Over the tall grass we could see some children playing around the houses. A dog must have caught scent of us because it started barking up a storm.

Suddenly a group of highwaymen came thundering out of the woods and surrounded us. Though it was almost dark, they looked like the same group who had been waiting on the far side of the river the day before.

Brother John must have been the most alert among us. He jumped from the wagon and took off running through the grass toward the village, yelling "Help! Help!" at the top of his lungs.

As a couple of horsemen started, a rider with a fully drawn bow and arrow pointed it at Doctor Luther and said, "Are you Martin Luther?"

"I am," he quickly responded.

"Forget the one running away," called the bowman after the two riders. "We got Luther here."

Brother John, with the riders right behind him, had nearly reached the village before they turned back.

"Get down. Get down out of that wagon," the leader ordered us. And to the others he snapped, "Take them both."

It happened so fast, and it was so dark, that I couldn't have told you at the time whether there were six or eight riders. But they soon had ropes around us and were riding off into the forest with us in tow. Only then did I notice some feeble cries coming from the village across the field. I looked back to see Brother John and three or four peasant men running toward us waving pitchforks and scythes in the air. I groaned. They would be no help.

Once among the trees, it took my every effort to keep from tripping over roots or getting slapped in the face by low-hanging limbs. Unable to move my arms because of the ropes that bound me, I was soon completely out of breath from running. I was surprised that Doctor Luther didn't fall down dead.

Once he did trip and
fall, and I tried to run
to his aid only to have
my tow rope whip me back and slam me into a tree.

Finally, our captors stopped in a small clearing.
There two extra horses waited. "Mount up," said the
leader. The ropes that bound us were untied and we
were assisted into the saddles.

"Here, drink this." We were both offered a skin
bag with fresh, cool water in it. I hadn't realized how
thirsty I was and took a long drink.

"Don't take all day," said the leader after we both
drank. He grabbed the bag and set off again through
the forest.

Among the trees it was completely dark by this time, and only when we were on a clear path or road with the trees broken above us could I even see where we were going.

We rode as fast as our horses could carry us, sometimes cantering, sometimes trotting, occasionally galloping. I had no idea how far we had traveled, but our horses were winded.

We finally slowed down to a walk and turned on to a road with two wagon tracks. A hooded rider pulled up beside me, and a low, youthful voice said, "We would have picked you up yesterday if you hadn't made that fool trip down the river. That wasted a lot of time."

What? It sounded like Arlene, but before I could be sure, another horseman came between us, and soon our pace picked up again to a trot.

Chapter 11

The Dark Castle

WE CAME OUT OF THE HEAVY FOREST onto farm land. The moon rose, and I was finally able to make out our company. Our captors always kept two or three riders behind us while the others went on ahead. I counted . . . four, five, six other riders besides Doctor Luther and me.

Now that we could see slightly by the moonlight, I noticed that we slowed down to a walk whenever we came near a farmhouse. *Maybe that would be a way to escape,* I thought. When we were near a farm, I could break for the farmyard yelling for help. But in a while I gave up the idea. What could one sleepy farmer do against six armed men?

But . . . were they all *men*? Now that I could see a little bit, I looked for the hooded rider who had spoken to me. One of the riders near the front seemed to be wearing a hood. I tried to work my way closer.

As we reentered the forest, I could only get glimpses of those around me when moonlight filtered through the canopy of trees. I pressed my horse to move forward. "Is that you?" I asked another rider.

"Who else d'ya think I am?" answered a gruff voice.

Embarrassed, I dropped back, but later tried with another rider only to be told: "Depends on who you were expecting." It was a man's voice.

Finally, I pulled alongside a rider who I could see in the occasional moonlight wore a hooded cape. Only this time the hood was thrown back and long dark hair flowed from the rider's head.

"Arlene! What's happening?" I demanded angrily, but keeping my voice quiet. A quick glance showed me that Doctor Luther was several lengths behind us. "Why have you ambushed us?"

"It's not an ambush," she said calmly, the pungent smell of our hot horses rising around us. "It's a rescue."

"A *rescue*?" I asked. "How could this be a rescue? And what did you mean about our escape down the river? How'd you know about that unless you set up those bandits to attack us?" I was determined to get some answers, but Arlene spurred her powerful horse, and it lunged ahead.

My head was swimming with weariness and confusion. What was happening? She claimed it was a rescue. But I felt like a prisoner, and it seemed more and more like Arlene was a spy for these night riders!

Within a short while we came to a halt, and everyone dismounted, apparently to rest the horses. In an instant Doctor Luther was at my side. "Karl," he whispered, "when I give the word, let's make a break for it. You ride just ahead of me. If we get into some deep woods again, try to hang back to create a space between yourself and the next rider. Then if there's a fork in the trail . . . maybe we can take it. Keep alert." Then he drifted away and began asking our captors for some water.

When we mounted up again, I maneuvered so that Doctor Luther fell in line behind me. And as we rode along, I hung back a little. But soon one of the men behind us called out, "Keep it closed up there." It had been the wrong place. I needed to wait until the trail narrowed and it was too dark for anyone to see.

But then I began to wonder: what if Arlene was right? What if this *was* some kind of a rescue? That's what she and the men who had recruited me back in Worms had planned. They were going to plan a rescue, and I was the insider who was supposed to help it succeed by keeping them informed of where Doctor Luther was and what he planned to do at any time.

On the other hand, Arlene had scolded me for our trip down the river. How had she known about it unless the men who had been waiting for us and this group were one in the same? If this was a rescue, maybe the incident at the ferry had been planned as one too.

I wrestled the question back and forth: should I trust her? or should we try to make a break? And then we came to deep woods again, and the trail narrowed and became very winding.

"This could be it," said Doctor Luther in a low voice behind me.

I started dropping back until there was one horse length, then two, and finally three between me and the rider ahead. "Keep a watch," muttered Luther.

I was keeping a watch, but was still uncertain what to do. *Could I trust Arlene or not?* The circumstances were all confusing. If this was a rescue, why didn't these people just come out and tell us what was happening? Of course Doctor Luther wanted to escape, because he knew nothing about any rescue plans. But . . . what if I helped him escape from people who were trying to help him? I tried to think what the options were. A wild dash into the dark woods. If we made it, we might get home to Wittenberg . . . but we'd still face possible arrest— not very inviting. Our other option lay with these strange riders and a girl who asked me to trust her. And suddenly I knew what my answer had to be.

The horseman behind Doctor Luther had dropped back just out of sight when an escape opportunity presented itself. Our horses were moving at a fast walk, and just as we came around a blind bend to the right I noticed that if one turned even more sharply to the right and ducked under some low hanging limbs, there was the hint of another trail that went steeply down into a ravine. Doctor Luther was close behind me and saw it at nearly the same time.

"That's it," whispered Luther.

I jumped my horse into the opening, but then I reined her in so hard that she reared up, whinnied, and almost threw me off backwards. I had acted on my decision to trust Arlene. I completely blocked any avenue of escape. Doctor Luther couldn't get by me even if he had tried to flee alone.

Hearing the commotion, the horseman behind us rode up and said, "That's not the way! Get back up here on the trail, and keep it closed up with the rider ahead of you. We don't want you getting lost out here in this forest."

"What's the matter with you?" said Luther through clinched teeth. "We had a chance, and now look what you did."

I didn't answer. I had made a decision. Now I would have to live with it.

Shortly we returned to riding on an open road, and there were no more opportunities to make a break from our captors. The road rose sharply as we climbed a hill, and then suddenly out of the gloom I realized that we were facing the walls of a great castle.

We stopped and the horseman who seemed to be in charge rode back along the column giving the message: "Silence! Silence. Our arrival is not to be known."

Then he went back to the front and whistled twice. A small light appeared in a tower, and soon I heard the muted clinking of chain. The drawbridge was being lowered for us.

We rode our horses one at a time over the drawbridge to keep down the noise. Inside the castle we dismounted and were met by a very large soldier. The moonlight glinted from his helmet. "Welcome," he said in a hushed voice. "I am the captain of this castle. Would you please follow me."

That voice . . . I was sure I had heard it before but couldn't place it.

The captain led us through several dark passageways and up two flights of stairs. The labyrinth was only occasionally lit by torches hung on the stone walls. The captain went first; Luther followed. From time to time I tried to pass so that I could get a closer look at the captain's face when he was in the light, but the halls were too narrow. Then the captain stopped by one torch. Below it was a box from which he took another torch and lit it. On we went into a

dark tunnel until the captain stopped in front of a ladder that went up through a trapdoor in the ceiling.

"Up the ladder, if you please, Doctor Luther," he

said as he handed Luther the torch. Just before Luther disappeared with the light though the dark hole in the ceiling, I got a glimpse of the captain's face. His voice was definitely familiar, but I still couldn't see enough of his face to place him. "You next," he said to me.

Doctor Luther gave me his hand to help me up through the trapdoor. "These will be your rooms," came the captain's voice from the dark below. "We're sorry they couldn't be more spacious. Tomorrow we can talk." Then he pulled the ladder down. The trapdoor was attached to the end of it, and soon it settled snugly into the opening.

I looked at Doctor Luther in the torchlight. I didn't know what he was thinking. But I knew what I was thinking. Had we been rescued, or were we in prison? It was hard to say, but there was no handle on our side of the trapdoor.

Chapter 12

Confined to the Tower

I AWOKE THE NEXT MORNING to the joyful racket of birds singing. When I went to the window, I discovered below us a sea of trees that swept away to a vast valley with a town visible in the distance.

I realized that Doctor Luther had come to stand beside me. "Quite a view, isn't it?" he said.

"I would consider it a more pleasant view to be on the outside looking in," I answered.

"Yes. Indeed. The question is, why have they brought us here?"

"I'd just like to know *where* we are."

"Oh, I recognize where we are, now that it is day. The town you see over there is Eisenach, where we were headed before we took our ride down the river. So this must be Wartburg Castle. I've seen it from a distance, but I've never been here before. I've heard, however, that it's a very strong fortress, not one a person can get in or out of very easily."

Our quarters were high in the wall of the castle, and the castle was on the peak of such a steep hill that approaching the base of the walls would itself be a hard climb. We occupied two rooms separated by an arched door so low that I had to duck to step through. Our furnishings were sparse: two narrow bunks, a small table, a writing desk, two chairs, and a chamber pot.

"The strange thing is," said Luther, "we're in Saxony, and this castle belongs to Duke Frederick. I have always considered him my friend—at least as much as it was politically safe for him to be. So why would he go against the emperor's guarantee of safe passage and attack us openly on the highway?"

The duke's castle? I tried to swallow the lump that was rising in my throat. "Do you think . . . I mean, could the emperor have canceled your safe passage early and ordered your arrest?" I said slowly.

"The emperor can do anything," said Luther with a shrug. "But if Charles has ordered my arrest, and if Duke Frederick has been so quick to do the emperor's bidding against me, I may, indeed, be without friends in high places."

"Except in heaven," I said.

"Right you are, Karl. Right you are." Luther chuckled. "Where has my faith gone? A little trouble comes and already I am forgetting who is in control of the universe." He once again surveyed the landscape that fell away below us. "Karl, this may seem like an impenetrable castle, but consider what a mighty fortress is our God. On earth is not His equal."

Just then a thud came from the square in the floor, and slowly the trapdoor rose. The ladder was put in place, and out of the hole emerged the bulky captain who had received us the night before. Behind him, of all people, was Arlene. Together they had brought us breakfast, bottles of water, and a pot of steaming hot tea.

"Have something to eat," said the captain. And then, as I got a good look at him in the light, I realized where I'd seen him before. "You're the man in the dungeon in Worms who tried to get me to report on Doctor Luther," I blurted.

"Yes, my young insider—Karl Schumacher, wasn't it? You've done a fine job for us, too . . . except for that unexpectedly long ferry ride."

I caught my breath. Maybe . . . maybe there was hope that I had made the right decision in not trying to escape last night. There was no doubt that this captain was the same man who had recruited me in Worms. He said it was for a "rescue." Arlene kept speaking of wanting to help Doctor Luther. Maybe I had done the right thing. But if so, why were we being held in this castle? Had they deceived me? I still wasn't sure.

Luther took a hunk of bread and a cup of tea and sat on the edge of the writing desk. "Please be seated," he said, indicating the two chairs for the captain and Arlene. I sat on the edge of the bed. Then with a very quizzical look on his face, Luther said, "What does this mean, Karl? You seem to know this man. And he calls you his 'insider.'"

"Maybe I should explain," volunteered the captain. "Duke Frederick has been concerned for some

114

time that you might not get out of Worms alive. That's why he worked so hard to get the emperor to guarantee you safe passage. But there's no predicting what this young Charles might do. He could cancel it any day.

"So the duke told me to arrange for your safety. He did not tell me what to do. In fact, he doesn't want to know because he expects to be questioned, and he wants to be able to honestly say that he doesn't know.

"I decided that the best thing would be to kidnap you. Common bandits or, more likely, men working for your enemies were a likely hazard on the highway. So we decided that the best kind of a rescue would be one that looked like an attack by highwaymen. Hopefully the emperor can be convinced that some too-eager churchmen jumped the deadline of your safe conduct and that, in fact, you are already dead."

I looked at Arlene. Her lips betrayed a small smile.

"But," the captain went on, "we needed an insider, someone close to you who could keep us informed about your comings and goings. So Karl, here, has been helping us."

"Did you know about all this, Karl?" said Doctor Luther.

"Not really . . . well, I knew about some of it. I did agree to help rescue you. But I had no idea about the ambush until Arlene told me what should have happened at the river . . ."

"You've been betraying me, Karl?" broke in Doctor Luther. "You've been telling these people where we were going and what we were going to do? How could you?"

"Wait a minute; wait a minute," calmed the captain. "Try to understand, Doctor Luther, that we have brought you here for your own safety. Even if you had gotten safely back to Wittenberg, it would have been only a matter of days before your safe passage would have expired and you would have been arrested. That is certain! And after that, only a miracle could have kept you from burning at the stake."

"Well, possibly so," admitted Luther. "But, Karl, how did you communicate with them?"

I felt relieved that it was all going to come out.

"Remember when we came through Duben and I told you that someone had been looking in our wagon, someone who went galloping off into the night?"

"Hmmm, yes. You thought it was that girl you had seen in Wittenberg, the one you called The Watcher."

"Well it was, and this is the girl," I said, pointing to Arlene. "She met me in Worms and arranged for me to tell her when we'd be traveling and where we were going. But what I don't understand," I said, turning to Arlene, "is, why you? Why a young girl out on the road alone?"

Arlene laughed. "This is my father," she said, indicating the captain. "And he was never *that* far away."

"Your father?" I said. "But why weren't you here at the castle, dressed in the fine clothes of a noble lady, learning the manners of court?"

"I have. I mean, I do want to learn those things. It's just . . ."

"Maybe I can explain," offered the captain. "My wife—Arlene's mother—died eight years ago. I have no other children, and I value Arlene's companionship. So I have undertaken to teach her the things *I* know: how to ride, how to shoot a bow, how to be resourceful. And she's become very skilled and courageous, don't you think?"

"Well, yes. But girls just don't . . ."

"Karl," said Doctor Luther, "certainly you remember Joan of Arc, the young French girl who led her whole country to victory in battle. There's a place for everyone with courage."

I reddened. What could I say?

Doctor Luther then turned to the captain. "I appreciate your rescue—I think. How long do I need to stay here?"

The captain cleared his throat. "I suggest that you remain in these rooms, unseen by the other people in the castle until your hair and beard grow out. Then you can have the run of the castle disguised as someone other than a monk. Without a disguise you are not safe from being reported."

Luther pursed his lips, thinking. I could tell he didn't like giving up his freedom to come and go, to teach and preach. "But as whom could I be disguised?" he finally said.

I suddenly had an idea. "This is a castle where fighting men gather. Why not be a knight . . . like you always wanted to be? You could be Knight George!"

Doctor Luther chuckled. "But I wouldn't be real. I'd be a pretender."

"So what? You need some kind of a disguise. And what's more common in a castle than a knight?"

"Just one more thing," I said to Arlene, still feeling a hint of suspicion. "How did you happen to be in Wittenberg at Raven's Tavern last winter? And how did John Eck know about Luther burning the bull only moments after you ran into the tavern, having seen it yourself? Did you tell him?"

Arlene's face went white, and her mouth hung open as she turned toward her father. Finally she took a deep breath and turned back to face me. "That was my big mistake," she said, wringing her hands. "I was staying there—my cousin owns the tavern. And my father and I have always been very interested in Doctor Luther. I saw you the day you took the bull off the church door."

"I know you did. That was the first time I saw you, too."

"Well," she continued, "on the day that Doctor Luther burned the bull and those other papers, I ran back to the tavern and told it all to my cousin. I didn't realize who John Eck was and that he was sitting right there and heard everything I said." She turned to Doctor Luther. "When I realized what I'd done, I decided that I had to help you. So I followed you to Duben, then came on to meet with my father. I'm so very sorry . . ."

"No bother, my dear," interrupted Luther. "It was a public event. Eck would have known within an hour anyway. You did nothing wrong."

Arlene looked at me, and we smiled at each other.

The days passed, not too unpleasantly, and I served Doctor Luther in every way I could. The first thing he wanted me to do was track down what had happened to our wagon and retrieve his Greek Bible and his lute. He decided to use his time in confinement translating the New Testament into German so the common people could read God's Word.

"But there's another way for people to learn the Gospel," he said to me one day. "We need songs, songs that the people can sing, songs that will stay in their hearts long after they have forgotten Sunday's sermon. How about this one, Karl?" and he picked up his lute.

> *A mighty fortress is our God,*
> *A bulwark never failing;*
> *Our helper He, amid the flood*
> *Of mortal ills prevailing.*

"I'm not sure what should come next," he said as he strummed the cords and hummed the melody again. "It's just that this castle with all its strength is really nothing without God's power. Here, how about this verse:

> *Did we in our own strength confide,*
> *Our striving would be losing,*
> *Were not the right Man on our side,*
> *The Man of God's own choosing.*

"And who is that?" I asked. "The captain of the castle?"

"No, no. But that's a good line. Hmmm . . ."

> *Dost ask who that may be?*
> *Christ Jesus, it is He;*
> *La, la, la, . . .*

He stopped singing. "Oh, well. I don't know yet what should come next. But I'll work on it. Someday, Karl, I'm going to publish a book of songs for the people. The Devil doesn't stay long where there is good music."

By summer Luther's hair had grown over his head and he sported a square, black beard. The captain gave him the run of the castle as Knight George, a visiting knight from some un-named land. And, indeed, Luther had been through some fierce battles, fighting for a powerful  Lord, defeating at least some of the evil in the land.

But in spite of his translation work on the New Testament, he always made time to help me with my studies. "You'll be ready to enter regular university by the time we get back to Wittenberg," he told me one day.

I grinned. My dream was coming true. But a new one was growing alongside it. It was about Arlene. We saw each other every day in the castle and some-times went for walks in the forest.

However, though dreams may keep you going,

they always have their obstacles. And my dreams about Arlene were no exception. At the end of the summer the captain sent her off to stay with his sister, the Duchess of Ebernburg, to be trained as a noble lady. I should have kept my mouth shut about Arlene not being trained in the social graces.

Oh, well. When she returns and I have graduated from the university, then maybe . . . .

More About
Martin Luther

MARTIN LUTHER WAS BORN on November 10, 1483, in Eisleben in Saxony (part of Germany). Soon after Martin's birth, his peasant parents—Hans and Margarethe—moved to Mansfeld to find employment in the mines. His industrious father rented a forge where he could smelt copper ore into raw copper and thereby went into business for himself.

Luther attended school there, in Magdeburg, and in Eisenach, and finally entered university in Erfurt. One day when twenty-two-year-old Martin was returning to the university, he is said to have been caught in a severe thunderstorm and nearly struck by a bolt of lightning. In terror he cried out and pledged to become a monk if only his life would be spared.

Within two weeks he made good on his promise and entered a monastery. In the monastery he made another vow: "Henceforth I shall serve you God, you Jesus, you only." And he did. On April 3, 1507, Luther was ordained a priest. His superiors found him to be very bright and dedicated. In 1512 he earned his doctor of theology degree and became a professor in the University of Wittenberg.

But in spite of his professional success, Luther felt tormented by his sins and did not feel he had found favor with God. The harder he worked to be "good," the worse he felt until one day he was studying Romans 1:17: "For therein is the righteousness of God revealed from faith to faith: as it is written, The just shall live by faith."

Even though he was a teacher of religion, he had not realized that one cannot *earn* God's favor. It is a gift from God, received by faith alone. And Martin accepted God's gift.

This discovery transformed Luther's life.

His first question was, "Why didn't I learn this good news from my church?" He looked around. Common people everywhere who wanted to please God were told by priests to buy indulgences and obey the church's rules. The selling of indulgences (written pardons for sin) brought much money into the church treasury. Obeying all the rules gave the church leaders great power.

Luther was upset. These practices were a fraud, and he decided to oppose them. He began by trying to convince the church leaders that they had to teach the truth. He debated other church leaders and wrote booklets saying why the church's practices were wrong. He declared that the Bible was more important than the popes or the declarations of the church councils that made up the rules. They were not supreme. They had made mistakes, proven, in

Luther's opinion, by the fact that they reversed their rulings on various issues.

A few church leaders and some state rulers agreed with Luther. Duke Frederick of the state of Saxony was one of those who sympathized with Luther. But other church and state leaders saw that his ideas could greatly weaken their power over the people, and so they opposed him.

As the story in this book relates, the struggle came to a head with Luther's trial at the Diet of Worms where he refused to take back what he had written unless he could be proved by the Bible to have been wrong. After his rescue and confinement in the Wartburg Castle, Luther remained there, disguised as a visiting knight for almost a year, attended by a young page who constantly had to remind Luther to remain in character.

While there he completed many influential publications, the most significant of which was the translation of the New Testament into German.

The Reformation was gaining momentum, but in some quarters, even in his own university at Wittenberg, it took a violent and fanatical turn. Luther was unable to give guidance from a distance, so he finally left the protection of Wartburg Castle to speak from the pulpit in the City Church in Wittenburg. His calming leadership was effective in Wittenberg, but the spirit of reform was abroad in the land. And by 1524 peasant armies were on the march against the wealthy landowners all over Europe. "We are free—it says so in the Scriptures. And free we will be!" they demanded. This was none of Luther's doing, at least not directly, but his ideas nonetheless sparked their revolt.

At first their vast numbers overwhelmed the nobility, and forty cloisters and many castles were taken. The peasants called for and needed Luther's support, but he did not grant it. In fact, he wrote a pamphlet encouraging the nobility to put down the revolt. They did, slaughtering peasants by the thousands.

Luther died in 1546, with the new church firmly established in Europe.

Though there were many reformers, several elements contributed to Luther being the most influential. He was a powerful speaker and writer and succeeded in publishing and circulating many of his ideas *before* he was forcefully opposed. This enabled him to enlist many supporters—some of them very influential. That may have saved his life. Luther's timing and location in central Europe offered a convenient issue for politicians in the Holy Roman Empire to use in trying to wrestle some of the power away from the Roman Catholic Church for their own purposes. Luther was not seen to be the threat to the state that some Anabaptists were because of their pacifism.

Initially Luther had no intention of breaking away from the Roman Catholic Church. He simply wanted to correct its errors. Therefore, it came as a surprise and a disappointment to him to find that his practice of a "reformed" religion in Germany had founded a new and separate church. He also did not want this church to take its name from him, but Lutheranism remains the name of the beliefs and practices he originated.

Today the Lutheran church—like many other churches—is made up of subgroups that operate differently from one another. Some adhere strongly to Luther's teaching that the Bible is the Christian's only rule for faith and life. Others place less practical emphasis on its supreme importance. Some teach Luther's discovery that our sins are forgiven as a result of God's grace, through faith alone, and that each person must exercise faith in order to enjoy a relationship with God. Others do not teach this clearly and offer more of a religion of tradition and ritual into which one is born.

For Further Reading

Bainton, Roland H., *Here I Stand: A Life of Martin Luther* (New York: Abingdon-Cokesbury, 1950).

Cowie, Leonard W., *Martin Luther, Leader of the Reformation* (New York: Frederick A. Praeger, 1969).

Fife, Robert Herndon, *The Revolt of Martin Luther* (New York: Columbia University Press, 1957).

Friedenthal, Richard, *Luther: His Life and Times* (New York: Harcourt Brace Jovanovich, Inc., 1967).

Lilje, Hanns, *Luther and the Reformation, an Illustrated Review* (Philadelphia: Fortress Press, 1967).

Severy, Merle, "The World of Luther," *National Geographic*, Vol. 164, No. 4, Oct. 1983, pp. 418-463.

Thulin, Oskar, *A Life of Luther* told in pictures and narrative by the reformer and his contemporaries (Philadelphia: Fortress Press, 1966).

Juvenile Fiction Series

From Bethany House Publishers

(ages 8–12)

Girls Only! · by Beverly Lewis

Four talented young athletes become fast friends as together they pursue their Olympic dreams.

Mandie Books · by Lois Gladys Leppard

With over six million sold, the turn-of-the-century adventures of Mandie and her many friends will keep readers eager for more.

Trailblazer Books · by Dave and Neta Jackson

Follow the exciting lives of real-life Christian heroes through the eyes of child characters as they share their faith with others around the world.